Feathers and Cigarettes

and Other Stories

This book is dedicated to
all of the writers who have entered the
Fish Short Story Prize since it began in 1994.

Feathers and Cigarettes

and Other Stories

Winners of the 2003
Fish Short Story Prize

Edited by Anne O'Carroll and Stephen Martin

Introduction by Pat McCabe

Series Editor Clem Cairns

Fish Publishing

Durrus, Bantry, Co. Cork, Ireland

Published in Ireland by
Fish Publishing, 2003
Durrus, Bantry, Co. Cork

This book is published with the assistance of The Arts Council and
Cork County Council

ISBN 0-9542586-1-4

A catalogue record of this book is available from the British Library.

Cover Painting, *Red Diva* by Ayelet Lalor
Cover design by Jula Walton

For details on Fish Publishing's Annual Short Story Prize see back of book.
Or write to:

Fish Short Story Prize, Durrus, Bantry, Co. Cork, Ireland
info@fishpublishing.com

Or see our website – www.fishpublishing.com

Contents

Editor's Note

When Aldous Huxley was asked what the prerequisites for an author actually were, his answer was firm and direct.

All one needs to write is paper and sharp pen, replied Huxley.

A sharp pen? queried the young journalist.

It needs to be sharp to open the vein, said the author drily.

It may be an apocryphal story, but it beautifully illustrates the respect that both of us, as editors, have for the efforts expended by *all* contributors to the 2003 Fish Short Story Anthology. The simple act of sending your work out into the world takes courage.

This year, Andrew Lloyd-Jones won the first prize of €1,500 for the wonderful *Feathers and Cigarettes*. The second prize, a week at Anam Cara Writers' and Artists' Retreat in West Cork, was won by Geona Edwards for *The Terrible Eyes of Big Hawkins*. This is the fifth year that this prize has been awarded and we are grateful to Sue Booth-Forbes for her continued association with the Fish Prize. We recommend a week or two at this unique haven for any writer. For the first time, we also have a third prize of €250, won by Katy Darby with *Pussycat, Pussycat*.

Fish Publishing is keen to help further the careers of writers, and to this end have commitments from literary agents Shirley Stewert (agent in the UK for Roddy Doyle), Merric Davidson, and Headline editor, Geraldine Cooke, to read the anthology with an interested eye.

There were over 1,800 entries to this year's competition. An enthusiastic editorial team filtered out the more accomplished for the first shortlist. Many thanks to Clem Cairns, Yann and Claire Kelly-Hoffman, Lorraine Bacchus, Tessa Gibson, Paul and Cesca Doonan, Geralyn McCarthy, Simon Kerr, Karen Kenny, Emily Muirson, Julia Fairlie, Francis Humphrys, Jamie Fisher, Carolyn Weese, Helen Kelly-Jones, Ailish Butler, Frank O'Donovan, Sarah Cunningham, Maggie Sweeney, Carmel Winters and Eithne Ní Mhurchú.

Our sincerest thanks to the judges, David Means, Pat McCabe and Geraldine Cooke, who selected the winners and runners-up for this book. Their sterling work and active support of new talent is greatly appreciated. Thanks also to John O'Sullivan and Mary Ross at An Post, Trevor Williams at www.traintrain.biz, and Sue and Gerald Hart.

Our job as editors was to distil a second shortlist for submission to the judges. Even so, dragging a literary drift-net through the initial selections was like being swept away by a very big wave. Each and every story was a tantalising glimpse into a writer's vivid inner world. There were stories of revenge and hatred, compassion and lust, trust and betrayal, loss and grief, whimsy and delight.

As the selections dwindled in number, things got very hot indeed. Co-editors' preferences differed and Solomon's choice had to be made more than once. Some stories were refreshingly original, but needed refinement. Many were very well written, but lacked the vital spark of unfiltered experience needed to kindle vitality. Others didn't make such a strong first impression, but snagged on the memory like a swatch of sheep's wool on a barbed wire fence and would not be dislodged. And every now and then, a story would swim into the mind like a glittering fish and take up residence there.

It was a privilege to select the short-listed stories. Our hope is that those who didn't make the final selection will continue to write and submit their stories, because the line between success and failure is ephemeral at best. We hope there is some comfort in knowing that our task was not an easy one, and that some stories were very hard indeed to let go of.

The anthology is launched at the annual West Cork Literary Festival in Bantry, Co. Cork. There follows a week of workshops, readings and other activities with established Irish and international authors. Traditionally, a large number of the writers in the anthology also show up to read from their stories. It is a unique chance for entrants to meet each other and other literary folk for some craic. Details on www.fishpublishing.com

Unpublished stories are uncharted waters. May you enjoy the adventure as much as we did because, as the ancient mariners knew, 'Here be dragons'...

Anne O'Carroll and Stephen Martin, May 2003

Introduction

Henry Thoreau said that it didn't have to be long but it would take a long while if you wanted to make it short. What was he saying this about? About the form we know as the 'short story'. Everyone over the years has had something to say on the subject. For V S Pritchett it was an athletic form. If you got a good start you could sprint to the end, unlike the nineteenth-century novel. For Frank O'Connor, it was the closest you could get to the lyric poem, in that the novel requires far more logic and far more knowledge of circumstances, whereas a short story can have the sort of detachment from circumstances that lyric poetry has.

Katherine Ann Porter wrote her stories in one sitting. Or so she said. But then writers say all sorts of things. Another thing that was said about the form – and I think it's a good one – can be attributed to William Trevor. That it's the 'art of the glimpse'. Meaning that if the novel is like an intricate Renaissance painting, the short story tends more towards impressionism. It is an *explosion* of truth and its strength ought to lie in what it leaves out as much as what it puts in, if not more.

O'Connor has said that for him short stories and plays go together – you take a point in time and develop it from there; there is no room for development backwards. Thomas McGuane made a similar point regarding the relationship between novels and movies, and I think it is pertinent to the story as well – in that, in the writing of screenplays you are conscious of the dangers of 'dead air'. You are not quite as willing to leave 'those warm-ups' in there, those pencil sharpenings and refillings of the whiskey glasses and those sorts of activities. You are very conscious of dead time, in the same way that playwrights are, or ought to be. Twenty mediocre pages, attests McGuane, won't even hurt a novel but in a movie screenplay they are fatal. You can't afford to hint at such slackness while writing a short story either.

P G Wodehouse said that his tales began in all sorts of different ways. He would start to write and in the process whatever it was he'd started off with got lost. On other occasions, stories would simply come out of nowhere.

Irwin Shaw, author of *Rich Man Poor Man*, said he loved its freedom. How it refuses to conform to any theory. Which would seem to render commentaries such as this one redundant. But perhaps there are, indeed, one or two constants. One of them being, as William Trevor has pointed out, that whereas the novel tends to imitate life, the short story is 'bony', and cannot wander. It is essential art.

This quality was uppermost in my mind while I was reading these submissions. I was looking for narratives where form and content were seen to synthesise perfectly, providing this 'essential quality'. As Trevor has written elsewhere, this 'explosion of art'.

But, most of all, I was searching for the 'new.' In the nineteen-seventies, the critic Alan Titley wrote a much-admired article entitled 'Not Another Irish Short Story!'

It was so devastatingly incisive that I remember going into hiding for weeks, my suitcases at the time being full of adolescent comings-of-age, not to mention any number of sagacious old farmers pondering their lives as the townland's lake swallowed up the local sun.

Lest anyone should think this is some sort of roundabout way of suggesting that what I was after were stories about 'Modern Ireland', and up-to-the-minute anatomies of 'Celtic Tigers', nothing could be further from the truth. I didn't care where they were set or what they were about but I wanted them, more than anything, to surprise or startle me. Astonish me, indeed.

For I think that was what Alan Titley was getting at – that the subject matter was in danger of becoming tired, and its treatment often as well. For me, the surprise tends to come from the style and when that happens I have to admit to being delighted. *The Terrible Eyes of Big Hawkins* was so accomplished it surprised me, sealed, as it were almost, completely within its claustrophobic and occluded world. Even if that world isn't entirely original, familiar as it is from any number of steamy Mason Dixon rural firecrackers. *The Last Elf-Mite* most definitely did surprise me, like some skewed but ordinary Harold

Pinter domestic episode eccentrically reworked by Isaac Asimov. I found it courageous and fastidious and unflinching in its courage. A writer well worth watching, I feel. But then there were many writers whose work came my way that I feel that this can be said about. *Mazes* was a very good, if quite traditional story, meticulously sculpted and without a single superfluous detail.

There was a lot of writing from America, I noticed, and much of it good, I have to say. But I would have preferred more recklessness here – initially, I mean – the shape can come later – and perhaps less of the admittedly excellent craftsmanship that seems to be the forte of the writing schools in that country.

What did surprise me was the manner in which much of the Irish writing approached its subject with an almost weary disinterest or knowledge of the society in which the story was taking place. One hopes that writers are not falling for this would-be deracinated, citizen-of-nowhere nonsense without which Gogol's Chichikov or Joyce's Bloom wouldn't have been half the men they were.

But, that said, there was much talent on view, and if I suggest that these writers should lock themselves in libraries, there to devour every possible tome on history and criticism and the politics of society, it is only because I think their work would be immeasurably improved. Especially now that the past has started to rumble and in far-off Mesopotamia the past has once again become the present as it has done, from Cheever back to Caesar and when Horace and Virgil were chewing their pens.

I would like to pay tribute to Fish Publishing for bringing this work to my attention and for providing writers with this platform. In a world where twenty screens of digital bullshit seem to be revolving without respite, cobwebs are gathering on majestic church organs and you can't turn on the radio without yet another irate 'taxpayer' complaining yet again about his 'rights as a consumer', there is nothing that can surpass the 'explosion of art' and its obstinate insistence on making sense of things, these dedicated scribes, as though some secret society, heroically, humbly, espousing a noble cause.

Pat McCabe, Sligo 2003

Feathers and Cigarettes

Andrew Lloyd-Jones

I couldn't go and Sarah Griffiths told me the next day that she'd seen Jason with some other girl at the Feathers and when I phoned him up, he was all like, I was never, and so I told him Sarah had seen him and he just said, it was nothing, chill, and I told him he was a bastard and that was it I'd had enough of his shit and he was all, don't be like that girl, and I was like, whatever, and hung up.

I phoned Sarah back and she was like, babes I'm sorry, he's such a wanker, and she said, let's go out, but I didn't feel like it and I didn't have any money anyway and so she said, her parents were out so I could come round hers, but her brother might be there. I said okay and told her I'd be there in half an hour.

I put on my tracksuit top from French Connection and my denim skirt from Miss Sixty and I pulled my hair back and did my eyes with Rimmel Planet Sparkle and my lips with Coffee Shimmer Exaggerate Hydra Colour just in case Jason or his mates saw me so I'd tell them I didn't need his shit any more and he could just fuck off and I was better off without him.

I took a fiver from mum and dad's drawer and I told my sister I was going out and she was watching something on cable and she said where are you going, and I was like, none of your business, and she said, it is my business, and I said, it's nothing to do with you, and she said, fuck off then, you look like a slapper, and I said no one would even look at you with all your spots, and she called me a cunt and I said, at least I've got one, and I shut the door as hard as I could on my way out.

Sarah lives about five minutes from me so on the way I went to get some cigarettes from the pakishop on the corner and the woman inside

1

looked at me funny when I said, ten Silk Cut and I stare at her like what are you looking at bitch and I just said again, ten Silk Cut, alright, then she turned and got me the cigarettes and I paid for them and walked out the shop. Some people never trust anything and that really pisses me off.

I smoked one on the way. I stopped round the corner from Sarah's house and sat on a wall and looked at the sky above the tower blocks and I thought I'm glad I don't live in one of them, that we've got a proper flat in a decent mansion block. The clouds were moving quickly across the sky and as I looked up at the tower blocks it felt like they were moving towards me, and that they were going to fall over. I finished my cigarette and flicked it into the street.

Sarah lives on an estate in a semi-detached house with its own garden and everything. I rang on the doorbell and she came down wearing her DKNY top and Diesel jeans and her gold Nikes that Darren bought her. She looked at me and gave me a hug and said, he's a wanker babes and I laughed and I cried a bit and she did too and I said fuck him, but I was glad she gave me that hug because it made me feel a lot better. We went upstairs to her room even though her brother was out and she put on the Groove Armada CD which always reminds me of when we went to Spain for the first time. Sarah's got loads of good stuff in her room. It's all right for her. Her dad's loaded. He's got a business in Thailand doing tours or something on boats and he's always going out there and bringing back stuff for Sarah, CDs and DVDs and duty free and that. I like going round to her place because she's always got something new but at the same time it makes me feel bad for my mum who can't always afford stuff like that now that it's just the three of us.

We sat there for a bit and talked about school and Mrs Brett who's making us all do this test on Monday and then Sarah mentioned Darren and I didn't really want to talk about Darren because she's always so loved up about him, it's like nothing he does is ever wrong or anything and it makes me sick sometimes, it really does. It's not like I'm jealous because Darren's a really nice bloke and everything, but it was just that I'd just broken up with Jason, and I didn't want to hear it then, you know?

Then her mobile rang and I knew it was Darren because of the special ring she's got just for him, which is that song Whitney Houston did that was in that film with Kevin Costner, anyway so it was Darren calling she answered it like hellooo, and then sat there talking to him and laughing on the phone, mostly just listening to him and laughing and talking like I wasn't even there and I was waiting for her to hang up and after a few minutes I was like, am I even here, because she wasn't going to hang up, so I said really loudly I'm going to get a glass of water or something do you want anything and she just shook her head and laughed at something he'd said.

I couldn't believe she was doing this, I mean, I'd gone over there she'd asked me over because I was upset and everything and the first time some fucking bloke calls she's all like, hi, and let's talk for ages and stuff. So I went downstairs and into the kitchen and got a glass and poured myself some water and drank it as I looked about the kitchen, opening drawers, seeing what I could find. Usually there's some money but there wasn't this time so I went to the fridge and opened it and there were some sausages on a plate covered in Clingfilm, all wrinkled and fatty and I took one and ate it. I'm trying to be a vegetarian at the moment but I was hungry.

There were three other sausages on the plate but instead of eating them I took them out of the fridge and looked around the kitchen. There was a pair of old shoes in one corner so I dropped the sausages in one of the shoes and shook them around for a bit. Then I put the sausages back on the plate, covered them back up with Clingfilm, and put the whole lot back in the fridge.

I went back upstairs and even before I got to Sarah's room I could hear her laughing and I knew she was still on the phone. I couldn't fucking believe it. I'd been down there like ten minutes I reckoned and she was still fucking talking or whatever to Darren. I thought about saying something to her but I was standing next to her brother's room so I decided to go in and have a look instead. One time I went in with Sarah and we found this pile of porn mags in a box in his cupboard underneath all these old board games and I thought it might be a laugh to see if they were still there.

His room was like all dark and smelled disgusting, like feet or something, all sweaty and fucking horrible. The curtains were drawn but I

3

could see he had all these pictures on the wall of like Jordan and Kylie and one of the ones from Hollyoaks, mostly pictures from Loaded and Maxim and most of them were like naked or whatever.

His walls were dark blue and he had a dark blue duvet and there were white stains on the covers and I went up to one of them and ran my finger along one and it was dry and crusty. His hi-fi was off but the display was on, like he'd just been in there or something and I thought I'd better see what I could find and get out before Sarah got off the phone if she ever would.

I went to his drawer and he just had loads of shit in it, like pens and screwdrivers and bits of watches and old headphones and some condoms and just shit really and I tried to find some money but all I could find was some strange banknotes from some country I'd never even heard of, I couldn't tell where they were from at all. So I shut the drawer and went to his cupboard and there were all these old clothes lying on the floor. And I found the box underneath boxes of Cluedo and Pictionary and Monopoly and I lifted open the lid being careful not to knock off the games and there weren't any magazines in it at all, just some more clothes, a shirt and some jeans. I thought there might be something under the clothes so I pulled out the shirt and that's when I saw there were these brown marks all over the shirt and I knew they were blood because they was the same colour my old knickers go when I'm on and I wondered why he kept this shirt in here all messed up like that and Sarah hadn't ever told me anything about him being in a fight or cut up or anything and then I saw this case at the bottom of the box. It was like a glasses case, kind of hard and stuff on the outside so I put the shirt back in the box and took out the case and opened it and inside there was all rolled up what looked like about twenty notes and it looked like they were mostly fifties and twenties. And under the money there were little folded bits of paper and I knew they were wraps and there was about twenty of them but I didn't know what was in them but I figured it had to be coke or speed. My heart was beating really fast and I looked around and thought fucking hell and I took a fifty and one of the wraps and stuffed them in my pocket then I put the rest back in the case and the case under the clothes and the clothes in the box and the box under the games and the rest in the cupboard

4

which I shut. Then I looked around just to see if there was anything I'd moved that I hadn't moved back and I stood there and looked at the girls on the wall and turned and walked out the door leaving it shut behind me.

Sarah was still on the phone in the room and this time she was talking really quietly and she wasn't laughing anymore and she was smoothing back her hair behind her ears and I knew they'd had an argument because that's what she always does when she's had an argument with Darren, talk really quiet like that and smooth her hair back. And I thought for fuck's sake and I sat there and looked at her for a minute and said are you going to be long and she just looked at me really pissed off and went back to Darren and her smoothing hair and I said I'm going to the loo and I took my purse and left her there talking quietly into the phone.

In the loo I put the seat down and got out the wrap and put it on the seat and knelt down and carefully unfolded the paper that had been carefully folded up, like it was like the love notes we used to pass around in class, all folded up in little triangles so that it folded in on itself and was all shut up tight. When I'd unfolded it there was this little heap of white powder and I dabbed a bit on my little finger like they do in the movies and tasted it and I knew it was coke. And smiling I got my debit card out of my purse and scooped a little off and put it on the loo seat and made it into a line. I've only done coke once because it's quite expensive and normally all we can afford is speed and it's usually all lumpy but this was really fine, all chopped up already. Then I rolled up the fifty and put one end in my nose and holding back my hair did half the line then switched sides and did the other half as well. Then I dabbed off the bits left with my finger and licked the card and put it back into my purse. I folded the wrap back up and put that into my purse as well between a book of stamps and this little card my mum gave me one time which has this story on it about someone walking through the sand and they leave some footprints behind and God carries them and there's only one path or something, I can't remember now, but it was a story I always liked. Then I had a quick wee before I flushed the loo and looked into the mirror and sniffed and rubbed my nose and the lights were really shiny and bright and made my highlights look really good and I smiled and looked at my teeth and then I took a deep breath and turned the light out and opened the door and

5

walked out into the hallway.

Sarah was sitting on the bed and the music was off and she was looking all upset and I said hello and you took your time and she said it's not my fault and I said you could have told him you'd call back and she said I think we've broken up alright and I just laughed and she said why the fuck are you laughing I'm not joking and I said you haven't fucking broken up you always do this and all you want is the attention just because I'm the one who's broken up and she said it's fucking not that and I said whatever I'm going and she said what do you mean you're going and I said I'm going and I stood up and grabbed my jacket and she said I can't believe you're going and I said well I am and I laughed again and I walked out the door and down the stairs and as I opened the front door I heard her saying I fucked Jason if you want to know everyone's fucked him as well you bitch and I didn't bother to shut the door behind me.

And I walked down the road and it was starting to get dark and it was a bit misty and the street lights were hardly there at all and I smiled again and I thought I didn't want to go home and so I just went for a walk. I stopped at the takeaway and got some chips and I thought about paying for them with my fifty but in the end I just gave him a pound coin because I didn't want to waste it in a chip shop, I thought I'd go up to town and use it in Top Shop or Mango or something instead in one go. I ate my chips and walked for a bit and then I realised I was in Jason's road and I walked down the road and there was no-one else about and his lights were on so I looked around and found a pile of bricks in another driveway under a sheet and I took the brick and I threw it at his window and almost before I heard it smash I was running running down the street the other way, away from his house and I didn't stop running till I'd got to the common and was sure no-one had seen me and then I stopped running and walked home the rest of the way.

When I walked by Jason's house the next day there was a big board up in the window where they'd covered it up and his father was outside sweeping up some glass on the patio outside the window. I watched him for a bit and then I felt a bit crap about the night before and so I went up to him and said alright Mr Buckley and he looked up and nodded at me.

6

Then I was all like what happened and he looked at me again and then he said someone threw a brick through the window last night and did I know anything about it.

And I said no but it might have been Sarah Griffiths who did it because when I was with her yesterday she took loads of drugs, her brother's drugs that she stole from his room, and she wanted to go over to Jason's house and fuck it up because of what she said he'd done to her and I said she was mad and I left and that was the last time I saw her but don't tell her I told him and I was only telling him that because I liked him and because of Jason, even though things weren't perfect between us now. And Jason's dad said thank you for telling me and he was sorry to hear about me and Jason but he was sure we'd work it out and he had to finish tidying this mess up right now but it was good to see me again.

And I walked off down the road and I turned around I saw him making a call on his mobile phone and I smiled to myself because I remembered I still had the fifty to spend and most of the coke as well and in the end yesterday wasn't that bad a day after all.

The Terrible Eyes of

Big Hawkins

Geona Edwards

Everybody knew it. The fool neighbors at the end of the road. The chickens in the yard. Why didn't I? There was scheming. That's clear. Oh bother. Just leaving that story alone, that's the best thing. I'd like to enjoy the peace of this evening before they stomp through: there's tornadoes afoot. I saw them in a cow's eyes this morning. No matter. I have already fallen.

Now that the sky's climbing over the back of the house like a sneak, the room's getting dark. *Git offa' me!* says the house. It's that kind of house. There's a candle in the corner reminding me of former times, times I never saw. I live in a place where there's still quiet. Still space. The sky can't surprise me, sneak though it is, 'cause I can see the whole damn thing out the back window.

I live in a place where the field you're standing in often goes right on out to the horizon, with nothing in-between but either wasteland or one single type of food, which some men collect and some men sell.

It's easy to get confused here. There's nothing to say what century we're in, not really. Jesus is still lurking around, so they say. God's country. I heard it so many times and I'm waiting, waiting, like they taught me. There's the patience of stones here. People keep expecting something gargantuan to roll over them, change the world up. Most of them'll wait forever. Me though, I'm starting to get notions.

My great-grandfather hung a great deal of black men from the oak in the backyard. In those days there was a lot of hanging. Now there's only the oak tree, doing no service, doing nothing. Waiting to fall.

There's something on the stove, making noise and giving this place a smell. Dinner? There's a metal ball in the bottom of my stomach saying yes. I don't recall starting up the stove, not exactly today. But I'll go on and believe it. It's a familiar sound, a sweet smell, and I remember starting up the stove on other days. The kitchen's not far away. It's a small place.

Great-grandpa. Grandpa. Pa. Me, and I had a son that was fat and too dark. It looked like Chinese pork. Rolled up, greasy. Fat little sausage face, it had, and fat eyes. Only two years in the world, and already those eyes were telling stories. Where'd you get them stories, sausage head? Why weren't them eyes empty like was only right? Empty till I filled them with whatever I saw fit, like any pa? *My* son would've grown to tear up a piece or two. There's a fact, you see. The men in my family make lots and lots of women pregnant. That's always been the case. Sowing the seeds. Sharing the wealth.

I can make the rocking chair move if I want to. My foot's up on the windowsill. If I push off I'll rock for about fifteen seconds, and then the chair'll have to wait till I push again. I like those little things that are all up to me. That only I can change. Another one is I can leave that stuff on the stove till it turns a kind of black leather, then eat it with a bitter face. Who's gonna' know? Nobody. Or I can leave it till it burns the house down. Why didn't I see it before? Damn it. Shame is not stood for in my family. Shit.

This window looks at the front yard, a long and lonely dirt road out to the mailbox, a falling-apart truck straight out of my grandfather's black and whites. Grandpa used to cry looking at those old photos. That used to shock me. I would be seven or eight or around that, and already I knew the face of a man was meant to be a serious place. Pa said, "A man crying is like an alligator forgetting his skin on the breakfast table." Yes, Pa, I said. "And your alligator wouldn't ever do that, now would he?" I shook my head no. It's funny though. I'm thinking now that I never had the slightest if a gator might forget his skin on the breakfast table or not. I mean, just one morning if he got late. But I knew what Pa meant. No crying. So that's how I got so surprised when Grandpa started weeping all over those photographs like a woman over her dead soldier. I guess he

9

loved those days of his childhood. Maybe he was missing when he used to watch those black men spin around on the rope. 'Cause providing you didn't care about the man, it might be a real bang-up spectacle, a circus bonanza, a genuine eye-popper. Imagine it for yourself, a body dancing up there with the bonfire sky behind it, out back around the oak tree. A beautiful summer night.

And don't mix my words. I don't want to see any black man spinning out back. Days are different now. But that's not saying either that I much care for those folk. Fact is, if the thing came down, hell, they could use my old tree, providing they had reason enough, and cleaned up after themselves. I'd damn sure insist that when I came out on the back porch for a stretch next morning – well, no beer cans or stray pieces of black man lying about. Oh dear. I do sometimes have a bloody mind. It's chow time. I got a hunger on me. Large. Look at that dust kicking up. Just look. Twisters. A cow's eyes don't lie, don't got that kind of choice. Not like a woman which is born to lie. Now what was it I put on that stove? Oh yes. I recall. Two eggs this morning. Let me just sit down now... there. Well! My teeth tear right through. Not surprising. Suppose it is flesh, after all. Overdone they may be. But still soft. Chew. Chew. Now... this is downright enjoyable.

When I finally got sleeping last night, it was like one of those spirit-guarding charms the blacks used to mess around with when their cabins fill up of moonlight. By that I mean the story following me around all the time had to quit when I went to sleep. Quit chasing me around, making me feel like a woman on the run. I slept like a dead fish, x-eyed. It was the only rest I've been able to get from that story. I've wished up and down it was a man I could punch in the face. Punch his lights out. Punch punch till his face was red mashed potatoes. But the story's not a man, it's a nightmare in my head. It's a nightmare that happened one night and won't let go, won't move on. Won't die. Like Big Hawkins. I'd have hated to meet that man.

Grandpa told me about Big Hawkins. His momma'd really named him Big. That was his name. The simple fact was that every last thing on him was not only big but abnormally humongous. This included his mouth and that's how he landed himself in hot water with my Great-grandfather and his crew.

One summer they were forcing black women down much more than was usual and tolerated. Some of them were even falling in love – an epidemic getting fast out of control. Anyway, no real problem, not really. 'Cause if the business came to light them whores were heathen temptresses who got what they deserved for wiggling out there in the fields like that, weren't they? I mean, wiggling before the eyes of white Christians. Case closed, right?

But Great-grandpa got sick in the head one time, and took a youngin' behind the workshed. He went into her ass. She was ten. When she started hollering Great-grandpa took a big rock and smashed the back of her head. Well she shut up quick then, but trouble was, Great-grandpa liked it. He liked the sound of the rock against the young girl's skull. He liked the red blood on the black skin, on the white shirt. He did it again and again. Smash, smash, the skull was changing shape. Oh, there was a fever on Great-grandpa that afternoon, all right. He shot off inside that young body, must have been way up in her guts or something, and she didn't stand a chance of still being alive.

Great-grandpa wiped his mouth, hurried off hiking his trousers up, and who do you think saw everything but Big Hawkins? Big was the eyes of those fields. And his eyes were huge too. Fat, bulbous bug eyes that drank in the world like a pair of wolves tearing at meat. Things got so nothing seemed to happen in those fields that Big Hawkins didn't see. It was scary sometimes. "Nonsense," said Great-grandpa. He called it darkie mumbo-jumbo to think Big Hawkins had any kind of power. He also knew Big was on loan at the Haines farm that afternoon, fifteen miles away.

But go figure, two days later, Big started talking, and he had details that left Great-grandpa's heart cold. Old man Haines swore all over his mother that Big never left his sight that day. So how did that old negro giant know those things? No matter. He knew them. And he said them. And nobody in the whole county, knowing Great-grandpa, could pretend to doubt a word of it.

But a black man has no leverage. What's the word of a black man worth? Thanks for the story, Big. Real entertaining. You just did yourself.

The posse was called. Big was found inside the hour. About ten scratchy-chinned white men tore him off that wailing mother of his. An angry procession of folks, shouting their heads off, made their way to the oak tree, dragging poor Big along the ground by a rope. That's how Grandpa remembered it.

They strung him up in the usual manner – only before they did, Great-grandpa gouged those giant eyes out with a soup ladle. Night had fallen, someone lit a fire, and up went Big Hawkins, eyeless, screaming, kicking like mad. "Jesus!" Great-grandpa was jumping around, wild-eyed, shrieking like a shot cow. "Christ in hell these eyes!" He had the orbs, one in each hand. He'd forgotten all about the hanging, and marched over to Grandpa, who was ten at the time, same age as the dead black girl. Grandpa was lingering by the porch, eyeing his ranting father, only freshly told about the thing with the girl behind the workshed. He was thinking of that. Thinking of that rock coming down on her head. Big told a good story. It went through a hundred people and still came to young Grandpa word for word.

The eyes were shoved into the face of the child. "Look at these eyes, boy! They're bull's balls!" Grandpa's told me what was in his head, face to face with them crazy big browns. That his pa was cracked. That those eyes were not got from a human being's head. That Big Hawkins was gonna' climb down from that tree after everybody'd gone home to bed, break into the house, find his eyes, and eat up the whole family, limb by limb. Grandpa told me he was sure about that last part. Maybe the fear he felt then was what put him a little on the Nancy side later on. I mean, crying at those black and whites and all.

Anyhow, Big stayed up there kicking and twitching and spinning for a good ten minutes. That dark leather neck of his was holding the rope off, you could see those bulged muscles working. That meant his lungs were full of air, just like he was on a stroll in the open countryside. And he wasn't scared either. He was steaming mad. That, Grandpa said, you could see in the type of lines his mouth made. Not panic lines. Effort lines. People below were starting to get ancy. A lynch wasn't supposed to go that way. A lynch was carried off in the mob's risen fire spirit, with yelling and cursing and foot-stomping. But now people were growing hoarse and tired. The lust went down. Got cold. A woman cried. That was a man up in that tree now. The crowd got quiet. Hearts got soft.

Great-grandpa was having none of it. He ran over to the fire just below where Big was dangling. He threw the mighty eyes into the flames. He snatched a rifle off somebody and finished the job. People traipsed away, heads hanging. On the whole, a night they wanted to forget.

Now I don't normally go in for this kind of thing, but Grandpa let me in on a peculiarity he believed he saw. That Big didn't die from no rifle shot. That all the lights in that great house of a man went out, that he stopped his kicking cold, soon as his eyes got gobbled up in those flames. Go chew on that some.

It's a story I often run through my head. It's long and keeps my attention better than most. Rough it sure is. But I came from that story. Direct. Like if one of them grizzly fellows who were there had turned his back on the mob for two shakes, long enough to hawk a thick wedge of spit into the darkness, outside the firelight. That's me. Born there in the warm spit. There's lynch-fire in my blood.

Now I was figuring this morning. And now that I know that whore – and good thing for her she's three states gone from here – now I know that whore what gave me that little sausage was letting blacks in off the back porch while I was working, taking them into my bed, receiving and receiving like nobody's business, whooping it up, getting animal in my absence – damn lucky for her she's out of my reach – now that I know what the neighbors and chickens kept from me, fuck 'em, what kind of serpent I had in my house, I was putting two and two together, figuring. And here's what I figured. That Big Hawkins was eighteen years of his age when he died, which means, knowing his kind, there was probably something like twenty little Bigs already running wild over the earth. And those little Bigs ran around till they were giants like their pa, then started getting up to all kinds of hell, answering tenfold each time nature called. I figured at least fifty grandsons came down from Big Hawkins direct, and how many more did them fifty spawn? Jesus. And not one of them, sure, went more than a stone's throw of these fields when they settled. Which means there's a high chance a load of seed come down from Big, the man himself, got shot right up into that pretending hellcat what called

13

herself my wife for a time. Shit. I was figuring this morning, over breakfast, looking at them fat story-telling eyes of the sausage child in front of me, that them eyes were no accident. That the flesh on him was darkly for a reason. Shit. Not in my house, friend. No sir.

The windows are speaking. Moaning. That's the wind kicking up so it is. That's twisters coming. I think I'll go out back and check on the rascal. Sure he's out like a light.

There he is. There's my boy. It's strange how the high winds just before a twister make such a racket, but somehow put a quiet on things. They shut the birds up. The cows and insects. The dogs yap away all right but the winds plum swallow up their small sounds. There's nothing out here but wind. Whistling. Humming. And then you got your things floating by. A scrap of cloth, a bag, hay, floating up there in all that whistling silence. The bag blows right up into your legs and you're waiting for the sound but it doesn't come. The wind drowns it. All you hear is the wind humming when it runs into things. And it's strong enough to swing a babe hanging from a tree, so it is. There's my boy. Big's boy. Swinging to, swinging fro, just like his great-grandpa before him, the one where he got his eyes from. But you ain't got those eyes now, sausage head, do you? What happened to your story-telling? (Shit. I'm shouting out loud to a dead baby with no eyes hanging from a tree. Shit.) Where'd your eyes get to, boy? I wonder. You remember them eggs I ate today? That's right. Now you just sit tight up there, sausage. We got twisters coming. And you're about to go for a little ride. You and me both. And that bejeesus tree. And the house.

Pussycat, Pussycat

Katy Darby

Always been big. Broad in the beam and the bone; a prop, a rock, a block-and-tackle heavyweight. A good man in, or preferably before, a fight. Just look at 'em, Sam, and they'll decide it's too much hassle. One of nature's bouncers. A trouble magnet for people looking to get hurt. Six foot and sixteen stone, someone you leave alone: I'm not worth it.

So at school I played all the sports I could, the ones where my size and strength gave me an advantage over the other guy. I was fast too; surprisingly so. Not elegant or graceful – I just have to walk into a room and the breakables start leaping off the shelves in pre-emptive hara-kiri – but speedy enough. I could run with a rugby ball as well as sit on my opponents until they gave up. I represented the county at shot-put, captained the school at American football. Not exactly the jock hero, me; never really had the looks for it, but I got by.

Aged seventeen I got ideas above my station. Auditioned for the school play for a laugh and suddenly discovered that I had, if not talent, at least something that could pass for it in a poor light. Discovered I enjoyed all that dissembling as well: speaking other people's words in a voice not my own. Playing the fool or the villain, or both. I read for Ferdinand in *The Tempest*. Anyone who went to the audition was excused assembly and all the boys were made to read the same speech, the one that begins "There be some sports are painful". i looked at it and agreed: I'd had my nose broken in a rugby game the month before. I never was much to look at, but it had still made a hell of a mess. So I read it through.

My stomach wowed and fluttered but I could hear my voice, clear and steady, echoing through the gym. "The mistress I serve quickens what's dead/And makes my labours pleasures." I had taken my glasses off and

15

stared sightlessly out at the audience, where the three teachers who sat in judgement upon us perched on black plastic chairs taking notes, a lonely island of humanity on the yellow pine floor. It was a minor miracle that I finished the speech at all: I'd never even thought of acting before. I walked off, trembling, to spontaneous applause from some of the younger boys. My friend Al took my place: he read, not very well, but in a penetrating, accentless voice with only the merest hint of a wobble. Al was my height but slender, with pale smooth features like sculpted ice. He looked like the picture of Keats in my volume of the *Collected Poems*. His hair curled like a Victorian virgin's. They cast Al as Ferdinand and me as Caliban.

Our Miranda – drafted in from the local girls' school, as a treat – was one of those pretty girls whose attractiveness is entirely bound up in their decorative qualities. Even back then I looked at her and realised that, with no personality to make them memorable, her even features would lose their prettiness, sunk in fat and petulance, by the time she was twenty-five. At sixteen she had a fresh, rosy beauty more striking because it was so tangibly ephemeral. She looked, walked, talked, sang like a well-trained doll. She would have made a wonderful debutante at any time during the last hundred years, as long as she married early, before her husband realised what a dull wife he was acquiring. Pretty Miranda's lack of acting talent was covered, mostly, by the stylised nature of the verse, which she learned parrot-fashion without understanding its meaning. Our director, Mr. Hall, spent weeks of rehearsal explaining to her what she was saying and what emotion he wanted her to convey, before giving up and simply providing a heavily emphasised line-reading for every speech. I still can't hear some lines of the play without Miranda's doll-tones chiming along in my head. "O *brave* new world that has such *people* in it!" Still, it worked.

Al was different. He'd been bitten by the acting bug too, and we worked on our scenes together, each directing the other and talking about our characters with the breathless enthusiasm which other boys reserved for discussing their football teams. He always got it almost right, but there was something missing: perhaps not maturity, because Ferdinand is a juvenile lead, a callow, romantic youth, like Romeo or Florizel in *The Winter's Tale*. Perhaps it was understanding, again; that essential spark that can set a speech on fire and dazzle audience and actor alike. I'd just discovered Keats and Yeats and the thrills of writing my own bad teenage poetry: Al had always been more of a physics-and-chemistry guy. We were two sides of different coins, but maybe that was why we got on. I ached for a new body to match the new side of myself I had discovered in the play. I would have given anything to lose the thick wodges of muscle, the dinosaur bone that anchored me so solidly to the ground, and be able to sprawl with Al's loose-limbed, elegant lassitude. No consumptive androgyne me, though, however much I coveted the look. I started to spend less time on the field and more on the stage. Our games teacher grew fretful and one of the second year boys told me that he had been seen raging at the heavens as the school dropped game after game. I didn't care. Although the nearest I had previously got to the school theatre had been as a spare body to shift scenery, I was in my element. I read Peter Hall and Stanislavski, *King Lear* and *Brave New World*. I dreamed at night of plunging through the woods, leaves splattered to my body, uttering Caliban's wild barbaric yawp.

We had a lot of trouble finding an Ariel. One of the third year boys, an impish, skittish blond kid who looked like a cherub and behaved like a poltergeist, was cast, but two weeks into rehearsal he fell out of a tree (one we were strictly forbidden to climb, naturally) and broke his ankle. So it was time to raid the girls' school again. Mr. Hall decided we would be better off with a slightly more grown-up Ariel, even if it meant that, due to the load-bearing weight of the flying harnesses, our airy spirit must be female.

I can hardly now imagine why, rampant hormones aside, I had been nurturing a crush on Miranda for much of the rehearsal period. Her prettiness was beguiling, but I had met dogs with considerably more personality. She seemed neither to like nor dislike me, keeping her distance with neutered politeness. Was it her reserve that made me believe she was hiding another, profounder, side to her strictly two-dimensional character? It doesn't matter, because as soon as Ariel joined us I had eyes, heart, life for no-one else. Al shared my enthusiasm, although not to the same degree. He agreed that she was "fit", but wavered a little when I went on to describe her as a living goddess whose hem I was unworthy to touch.

"Why would you want to touch her hem?" he asked, a late-Romantic crease of puzzlement crowning his aquiline nose. Ever the literal-minded physicist.

"It's a figure of speech," I told him. "Hem, hand, heart, whatever. I'm her slave! Like Caliban is Prospero's. A bondsman to her beauty."

Al slurped his coffee and looked around the canteen with alarm.

"Steady on mate," he warned. I smiled the secret, pained smile of someone ridiculously and hopelessly in love.

Hope's a horrible thing. I've tried to stifle it at birth since that year. I've smothered it like a lingering relative, strangled it like a Christmas turkey and drowned it like a sack of kittens, but up it always pops, just when I think I'm free of the disease of optimism. Pope was right: it does spring eternal in the human breast. The breast would not be human without it. It is not a sad thing to love without hope: we all do it. Teenage girls worship boy-bands whom they will never personally meet, who are twice their age and probably gay to boot. I myself had a soft spot for Madonna in my youth, not to mention Emily Brontë, and she's dead. This is puppy love, pure fantasy, the stuff that dreams are made on. The cruellest thing is to nurture love of the tenderest, most breathless sort, for someone you actually know. Someone you see every day, in good moods and bad: someone you work and play with, someone whose crosswords you finish and lines you know as well as the back of their slender hand – that's the bitch. Her name was Amy, and with the slant of a glance or the twitch of her lips she could make me grin or cry for the rest of the day. I used to lie in bed feverishly composing French poetry in my head, which span with Rimbaud and the *Fleurs du mal*. I was fascinated by her name: how close a homonym it was of the French words for both angel and soul. Amy, *mon ange, mon âme, je t'aime ...*

She was clever; perhaps even cleverer than me, and I'm no bag of hammers. She was that rare and wonderful breed, a scientist with an

18

instinct for the arts. She was doing maths and physics A-levels but she was almost as well read as I was and could have done English as a fourth subject without breaking sweat. She just had one of those brains. A Renaissance mind, I called it one day, and she was so pleased that she let me finish her cigarette while Al looked on in nicotine-deprived longing. We were in the little clearing in the woods behind the gym which countless generations of schoolboys had marked with their territorial spore: carved names and bark stripped from the dead trunk of the smoking tree, orange butts trodden ten deep into the forest floor. I figured then that smoking a cigarette which had been between her lips was probably the closest I was ever going to get to kissing her, and was blissfully content with that. Little did I know.

She liked poetry too. It was cruel, almost, how much we had in common, considering that for all the chance I stood of deepening our relationship we might as well have been living on opposite sides of the sun. She had a surprising penchant for Sylvia Plath, telling me with gossipy excitement that the first time Plath had met her future husband, Ted Hughes, at a party, she had gone out of the room to kiss him and come back with a great bite down her cheek. She brought in the poem "Ariel" to rehearsals one day, to show me. She read it out between drags on my cigarette and I agreed that it was beautiful, but I was frustrated by my inability to comprehend it. Usually I went after a poem's meaning like a ferret down a rabbit-hole, and came back up very pleased with myself, with some still-warm prize of subtext clamped between my eager jaws, but not this time. I wondered if it was because the poet was a woman. Were there modes of expression, wells of experience I simply had no access to because of my gender? How come I could appreciate the form but remain baffled by the content? Of course, that's a pretty good analogy for most adolescent boys' relationships with the opposite sex, but I considered myself better, deeper, brighter than that. I was as disappointed as she was by my failure of understanding, until she mentioned casually that the poem was dedicated to Plath's horse, and all the talk of wild riding and flowing limbs made sense at last. That was my first and most important lesson in understanding literature, not to mention people: however seemingly complex or incomprehensible, everybody and

19

everything has a key, a code or clue with which you can start to solve the mystery of them. This is why yes can often mean no: this is the secret language in which "I'm fine" translates as "Help me".

A week or so before the performance, I wandered into the dining hall and approached my usual table to find Amy poring over the crossword with Al. I was slightly taken aback at his usurpation of my traditional pen-biting place at her side, but Amy explained he was keeping her company until I got there. She twisted the paper round so that I could see it. I gave it a cursory glance, forking scrambled eggs into my mouth.

"Sixteen down is humdrum." I tapped the grid with my knife. She obediently filled it in with wobbly upside-down letters, not wanting to break the spell of my concentration.

"Twelve across, orrery. O-R-R-"

"It's OK, I know." She gave me a conspiratorial little glance through her eyelashes as she bent to write it in. My chest hollowed and filled again with hot champagne.

Al, amusedly bored, was folding a bird out of his paper napkin. He always was good with his hands. He had built a bong of quite startling beauty and efficiency out of old lab equipment the term before, which still gave us both many hours of pleasure and use. He flapped the bird over Amy's head as she stared at me, watching me ponder seven across. She waved it away, not breaking her glance, smiling.

"Get off me, origami freak."

Al cooed like a dove. He made fluttering sounds as the bird settled on the glossy sweep of her hair. She screwed her nose up.

"Schopenhauer," I said.

The dove dipped its paper beak and began to forage in the crevice of her ear. Amy squeaked.

"Get *off*! It tickles!"

I snatched the pen from her twitching hand and filled in the clue myself, inking hard over the previous attempt in Al's neat scientific lettering. They were both too embroiled in trying to gain control of the dove to notice.

"But it *luuuurves* you," Al was cooing.

20

"You've made a fucking mess of this," I told him in my hateful angry voice, the one that goes high and out of control in the moments I most want to be *basso profundo*. I don't think they heard me. "I can't do anything with the rest of it," I said, louder.

The dove swooped under Amy's chin, Al's coos mingling with her yelps. I reached out and grabbed its paper neck, crushing the bird into a tight ball in my big fist and dropping it on the table between them. They stared at it with identical hurt, disappointed expressions, which annoyed me even more.

"Pigeon pie all round, then?" I said with a tight, precarious grin, and left the table. I didn't want the rest of my food. I took off my glasses and cleaned them fiercely on my rugby shirt. I couldn't see where I was going with tears in my eyes anyway.

The scene we were rehearsing next day had always been my favourite: the one where Ariel confuses the drunken Caliban and his new masters, Stephano and Trinculo, by intervening invisibly and repeatedly in their conversation with a mischievous "Thou liest!" I had always wanted to try the scene actually drunk, and my hurt heart and a bottle of cider from the local village shop (which had been selling me alcohol unquestioningly since I was fourteen) provided me with the perfect opportunity. I knew the lines backwards and upside-down so I wasn't worried about drying, but I wasn't prepared for the emotional effects of drunkenness. I can be pretty maudlin at the best of times, and this certainly wasn't one of those.

Stephano and Trinculo were a couple of boys from the year above, also members of the rugby team, and when they discovered me in the dressing room covertly and miserably choking down my bottle of Woodpecker they thought it was a brilliant joke, and insisted on joining in. They shared the rest of the bottle between them, and being more used to drinking than I, by the time we took the stage they were merry but not trashed. I had been self-consciously indulging my misery by not eating, so I was barely able to stand, and for the first few minutes this made for a superbly funny scene. When Stephano commanded me to kneel and swear fealty to him I collapsed on my knees with a deafening crash, and a crack that only I heard, which meant my football injury had popped out again. Writhing in genuine pain, I told them how Prospero had cheated me of my island.

I could feel Amy enter behind me: her light step was inaudible, but I could always tell when she came into a room. Love, and alcohol, make us sensitive to such things.

"Thou liest!"

I struggled thickly on through my lines and moves, lumbering across the stage to catch the invisible voice, as each cat-calling repetition infuriated Caliban more and more. I could feel the fury and sadness building in me like nausea as Amy darted away from me, teasing and tickling me like a paper dove, always just out of reach. I began the speech about killing Prospero, imagining Al's face as I exhorted them to "Batter his skull, or punch him with a stake/Or cut his wezand with thy knife." No need for me to imagine what a wezand was. Caliban told his inebriate lords to burn Prospero's books, "for without them, he's but a sot, as I am." He dangled the carrot of Miranda's beauty in front of their drunken donkey noses.

"This will I tell my master!" Ariel exclaimed from right behind me, and I wheeled round and hit her.

Everyone went silent. Mr. Hall went purple. Amy went white, but for a bright red blush on the cheek I had hit. I dropped to my knees and heard that horrible crack again. We were on the same level now, she staring blindly ahead, touching her face gingerly like it was covered in wet paint. I crawled towards her – a foot, no more – and she shrank back.

Mr. Hall bounded up onto the stage in a great, athletic leap. I suddenly noticed that, despite his gentle, shambling-bear demeanour, he was even bigger than I was and a hell of a lot angrier. He took Amy gently by the shoulder and looked at her bruising face.

"Al, you're not on for a while. Take her to see the nurse, would you? We'll take a break. Are you all right to walk, Amy?"

She turned that same hurt, disappointed look on me. I felt the dove crush in my fist.

"I'm fine," she said numbly.

In the corridor Mr. Hall pointed out to me that, given the variety and

22

severity of my crimes, I was extremely lucky not to face expulsion from the school. As it was my parents would have to be informed. I didn't listen, catatonic and exhausted by the shock of what I had done. I said again and again that it was an accident, an accident. I couldn't say the word *sorry* enough. I wanted to be given lines, to write it out a thousand times until it stopped cramming my throat and choking me. I couldn't even cry. My mouth was dry and all I could think about was the livid colour of her face where I had hit it; the print of the monster's fist.

When I visited her in the infirmary the funny thing was that she seemed to pity me more than anything. She knew it was an accident, she said, fingering her blue cheekbone, smiling awkwardly through the bruise. I hadn't even hit her square on, I was just flailing around. I must have been pissed. She could smell it on me. I claimed feebly that it was Method acting; worth a try. This wrung another lumpy grin out of her.

"It's all right," she said. "I know you. You wouldn't hurt a fly."

She was wrong. A fly I would have hurt. I would have slaughtered an army of anything from bluebottles to Bolsheviks for her sweet sake, but I would never, ever have dared to touch her in love, let alone anger. My blundering body had betrayed me again. Her kindness hurt me more than screams and blame could ever have done. How could she not understand that I appalled myself: that she should be appalled, too?

"Hey, cheer up! It's not that bad."

But it was. It was. I couldn't trust myself to speak. I covered my trembling mouth with both hands, staring mutely at her. She gazed back in astonishment.

"Oh dear, you're feeling it worse than I am. You're just a big pussycat, aren't you?" She reached out and stroked my hair, at a loss how to comfort me. Meaningless words of apology throbbed in my throat.

"I'm fine," I said helplessly. "I'm sorry. I'm sorry. I'm fine."

When Al came in to take her back to the rehearsal, he didn't even look at me or register my emotional collapse. As he shut the door behind Amy he cast a single word at me, like he was lobbing a stone at a cat.

"Twat," he said, succinctly. I couldn't deny that it was the *mot juste*.

When I remember the last-night party – and Christ and the angels, how I remember the last-night party – I sometimes wish I *had* been drunk. In my varied experiences of drinking since, I have always found it hard to predict whether alcohol will numb or enhance the pain, but I can hardly imagine that the pain of that night could have been sharpened, however hard I or she had tried.

Although the cast, as a special treat, was allowed a strictly controlled intake of alcohol, and smoking was turned a carefully blind eye to, I was under the severest injunction from Mr. Hall not even to look at a can of beer. I didn't want to: the sight of the booze and the memory, still faint on Amy's flesh, of the bruise, sickened me. We had reconciled, in a way, during the show's run, but I felt as though I had broken something in our friendship. Al had also appointed himself as her protector, ridiculously: I could have snapped him in two if I had wanted to get to her. We barely spoke, he and I. Even though she had forgiven me, he wouldn't.

All this meant that I spent the night in razor-sharp, razor-bright sobriety, watching Al and Amy dancing and laughing while Stephano and Trinculo got pissed and rowdy, and the littler kids messed about and tried to cadge cigarettes off them. Miranda (even now, to my shame, I can't remember her real name) knew nobody apart from Amy, and so stuck with me for most of the evening. We sat out dance after dance, me darting glances at the happy couple in the corner, she prattling on about whatever occurred to her. She could talk, I'll say that for her, and I, sunk like a Spanish galleon in an ocean of speechless misery, proved a good listener. Everybody says that about me now. It's my virtue and my curse. Sam's such a damn good listener. No choice but to listen, when you can't say what you want to. Not, of course, that I had nothing to talk about that night: there was just nothing I *could* say.

The festivities, such as they were, were officially ended at ten o'clock, and we were all sent on our ways with strict orders to be back in our dorms by the eleven o'clock curfew. Amy and Miranda were being picked up by Amy's dad at eleven-fifteen, which left us all an hour or so to continue the party elsewhere. Stephano, Trinculo and Prospero led the way to the late-night smoking den in the woods: they had managed to blag or beg a bottle of wine from somewhere and everyone but me drank from the bottle, excited by their own mild intoxication. Miranda stuck to me like a burr. Al and Amy conferred privately over a shared cigarette. Hell had nothing worse to offer, or so I thought. We started to play that oldest of adolescent games, Spin the Bottle: after a few no-gos which paired Stephano and Prospero, then Amy and Miranda, the gaping neck pointed first at Amy and then, with dreadful irony, at me. A cheer went up from the rest, hastily shushed by Al, who was watching with languorous interest to see what would happen.

"You've got five minutes behind those trees," he said lazily, sure of his possession of her. I could not have hated him more. I looked at Amy.

"You don't have to, Amy. It's a stupid game."

But she was fired with the spirit of adventure: too drunk and careless to back down, however disgusted by the idea she was. She grabbed me by the hand and dragged me, stumbling, behind the copse. I could hear the laughter and banter of the others as we disappeared.

She turned her face up to me in the moonlight, filtered by the hushing leaves above us.

"At least this way we get a chance to talk," she said. "You've been avoiding me all night."

I stared at the wet leaves at our feet, not daring to look into her eyes.

"I'm sorry," I repeated. It seemed to be all I could say these days.

"Don't be. I'll tell you a secret."

"What?" I could hear Al repeating a joke to the others, something obscene I wasn't sure he understood.

"I didn't really fancy you before, but I do now."

"What?" I could barely believe I was hearing those words from anyone, let alone her, not after what I'd done.

"It wasn't exactly an accident, was it? Not entirely?" Her eyes were bright with moonshine, gazing intently into mine.

"Of course it was!"

"You were jealous of Al, weren't you? His stupid bird thing. You thought he was flirting with me. That's why you got drunk and hit me."

"No!" Even I didn't believe it, although it was true. How guilty must I sound? What was she doing?

"He's just a little boy. A little girl. Thinks I'm a little girl too."

"I just – he was treating you like a child – he doesn't respect you –"

"He was just playing. Anyway, I'm not so respectable."

She leaned in to me. Her lips were open. She was fingering the faded print of the bruise on her cheek, digging her nails lightly into the yellow flesh.

"Hold my hands behind my back."

"What?"

"You're a big boy, you can do it. Come on. I can't stop you, can I?"

I felt like the blood was draining out of my body. What was this sickness? Was she trying to have her revenge on me? Had she still not forgiven the unforgivable?

"I – I can't."

She turned her injured face towards me, where the marks of her fingernails formed a reddened semicircle like a human bite. She grabbed my hands angrily and clamped my unresisting fingers around her wrist, twisting our arms savagely upwards. Her breasts lifted and pressed against my chest.

"Why not?" she whispered. I could smell the wine on her breath, sweet and dreadful.

"Amy, no, you're drunk, what are you doing?"

"What's your fucking problem, Sam? You weren't so shy when you were beating me up on stage, were you?" Christ, the shame spread over me like fire.

"I'm so sorry about –"

"Don't be sorry! You're always so bloody sorry! Why don't you do what you want to for a change?" Her voice shifted. "Don't you want to?"

God, yes, but not this way. I wanted to brush my fingers over her lips, to kiss her eyelids, to collapse at her feet on broken knees. She stared at me, beautiful and pitiless.

"Don't you?"

"Amy – " I couldn't explain. "I love you."

Her eyes narrowed. Words in a foreign language.

"I can't. I love you." Tears were spilling from me, sober as I was. I folded my large hand over hers and gently brought it down, pressed it to

26

my chest. My heart was bludgeoning my ribs. I could hear it as though from a mile above the earth. She disengaged her fingers, looking at me with pity and disgust; or perhaps it was understanding, at last.

"Oh dear." she said mildly. "I've got you all wrong, haven't I? You *are* just a pussy in wolf's clothing." She stared at me for a moment, then slapped me so hard that my ears rang. I hardly felt it.

"You're not even going to hit me back, are you? All that muscle and you're too scared to use it."

I reached out to her again, and she slapped me away, even harder.

"Don't touch me."

"Time's up!" screamed the others from the charmed circle of wine and smoke. I stared wordlessly at her. I could hear the splash of my tears on wet leaves.

"Christ, you're pathetic, aren't you? Like a drowning kitten. I suppose I'll have to make do with Al after all. He may be a little boy but at least he's not frightened to touch me."

She stroked my hair roughly as she stalked off, pushing my head back so that I was staring at the sky.

"Poor pussycat," she said with contempt, and then she started giggling.

I could hear her still laughing and gasping as she stumbled back towards the others, as the starless black sky swam above me. "Meow," she was sneering under her breath, between hiccups of laughter. "Poor poor pussy. Poor pussycat. Meow."

27

All Bones

Mia Gallagher

Dark. Sweaty. Bass pounding. Bodies heaving. Overhead arched windows, looking out onto black. In the centre of the dancefloor Neil knelt down, seeing a thousand stars humming a song of eternity. He was out of his face on acid.

She was in the corner, moving like some crazy fucked up disjointed mannequin. Her shaved head glowed sick green in the bad disco lights. She was all bones. The light changed green to blue to red to white, turning her from sea-creature to madonna to devil to skeleton.

The thought made it happen.

Her eyes stared at him, empty black holes. She began to move towards him.

Coming to get you.

She slid her way across, slipping between the other bodies lumbering rhythmic on the floor, so thin that to his tripping eyes it looked like she was melting between them, coating them with a transparent patina of girl.

She was in front of him. Cheekbones like stone age artefacts, eyes huge and hollow, thin thin thin hands, waving fingers like seaweed. She danced like a maniac, elbows, hands, knees everywhere. Her rhythm was off, kept catching him by surprise, but slowed down by the acid, he enjoyed the sudden shifts, went with them.

Outside, she mouthed.

He followed her through the ecclesiastical passageways of the deconsecrated building. She came and went in the darkness.

"Wait!" he kept saying. "Wait for me!" Except he was so out of his face he couldn't tell if he said it out loud or not.

She drew him into a room filled with red light and angular mechanical objects, sinks, plastic bottles full of dark liquids. *Alchemy*, he thought. *Far fucking out.* She waved a key in his face and kicked the door shut behind him.

How the – he began to think, then stopped as she placed her mouth on his like a wet soft hand and dug her tongue in.

She was voracious. Her lips were full and wet, soft cushions. They belonged to a fat girl.

Down, down onto the ground.

"Hey, easy," he said at one point, distracted from his orgasm, from the feeling of it, which he wanted to savour because usually you don't you know, but this time, with the acid he could, because it was so... except she kept fucking bouncing, like a Duracell rabbit on speed.

"Easy."

She stopped. Shame flooded her face, in the acid bath of his head distorting her into something by Goya.

"Come live with me," she said. Come fly away.

She lived in a tiny house in the inner city. Red-brick, two-up, two-down. Or in this case, one-and-a-half-up, two-down. She was very practical about it. That surprised him. He'd expected her to be more... demanding.

But no, she explained. Her flatmate had just moved out and she needed somebody to share with because she couldn't afford it on her own. She was a photographer. On the dole, no money, living off favours and other people's darkrooms.

Neil needed a place to stay. His ex had chucked him out, rents had exploded and there was no way he could afford somewhere on his own.

"Okay," he said, still dubious at the way she'd dug his mobile number out of thin air.

"Don't worry," she said, exhaling cigarette smoke from the corner of her mouth. "I won't bite."

She was American, Kentucky originally, but years of hustling in New York had eradicated any trace of a Southern accent. She presented herself as

29

being tough as nails, as an old boot, as something that had been left out in the rain for years.

He was given the bad room, the half-room, the one she had to walk through on her way downstairs each morning. She had the front room, the whole one with the big window and the floorspace and the ten strong wooden shelves.

She owned nothing. No pots and pans. No plants. No pictures. One day Neil stuck up two posters on the landing wall. When she saw them she turned sour, resentful, as if he'd walked in on her while she was asleep and pissed on her bed.

One afternoon, when he was bored and sick of watching *Jerry Springer* and *Stop Police!* re-runs, he decided to poke around. She was out on an assignment, meeting friends, something intense. All her appointments were loaded with the same intensity.

He poked his head around the thick black curtain that worked as a door between their rooms. He couldn't get over how empty her space was. No clothes, apart from a functional shoprail of baggy grey and black workwear and a row of heavy clunky boots. No ornaments, no girlish things. In one corner a tripod and three cameras, arranged like precious heirlooms. In another, a grey filing cabinet. It was as bleak as a prisoner's cell, he thought, somewhere a monk would sleep.

He wondered if he should go in. Why not? It wasn't as if he was going to steal anything.

The shelves were full of hard-backed folders containing slides. Nothing interesting, just her work; landscapes, cityscapes, her own body. She was obsessed with her body. He tried to open the filing cabinet, hoping to find diaries or some other evidence of who she really was, but it was locked. He gave up and was about to go when he saw a scrap of paper sticking out behind the edge of the cabinet. It must have dropped there but she hadn't bothered picking it up.

He teased it out.

A round-faced all-American teenager, sitting on the back of a big red Cadillac, big yellow fields stretching behind her. Endless America. She had apple-pink cheeks and curly brown hair that fell in spirals down to her shoulders. She was a big girl, strong and fit but definitely on the large side. Her arms were freckled, her face glowed.

Later that evening when she came in, moody and sour because her meeting hadn't gone well, he searched for the farmgirl in what she was now. He couldn't find her; she was long gone, reduced to almost nothing.

They fucked again from time to time, mainly when they were pissed, but never in her bed. The cheap uncomfortable sitting-room sofa, the kitchen table — a clumsy experience that left him with a black eye after he knocked a saucepan off one of the shelves — and his small, single bed. She bounced on him like a demon, urging, all bones. Turned off, he usually came close to losing his hard-on, except then he'd think of something — a gash mag, the girl in the Smirnoff Ice ad (undressed, of course), ex-girlfriends, the sweetie from his favourite café — and freed from service to the untenable moment, would come.

She never did. Nor did she pretend to. He wondered about that, but never for too long. It wasn't something they could talk about. One night when they'd been smoking grass, she opened her mouth and he thought she was going to say something. But he'd come, was in a world of his own, pleasant, warm and sated, and not really in the mood for going into all that. She must have read him because, instead of talking, she reached for the grass and rolled up another joint instead. And that was that. He didn't feel bad about it. He got the feeling it was easier for her not to go there; that way she wouldn't have to dissolve the wall of transparent ice she'd built around herself.

She ate nothing. Okay, not quite nothing, but as far as Neil — born and bred on rashers and eggs, beans and chips, hot dinners, chocolate, junk food, anything as long as it would do the job — was concerned, it was sweet fuck all. She ate bowls of steamed fruit first thing in the morning, followed by some mess of cereal you wouldn't give a dog. Salad during the day. Rice and vegetables, occasionally, at night.

One night when he was jarred he mentioned, jocularly, that she could do with some fattening up. She went stock still, the fag at her mouth seeming to freeze too, even its smoke frozen in mid-air.

"Oops," he said, trying to joke his way out of it. "Touchy subject."

31

She extracted the fag and blew a stream of smoke towards the telly. He noticed that her fingers were shaking. She didn't say anything, just zapped to Channel 4.

The next night he went clubbing and brought another girl home. The sweetie from his favourite café. She was lithe and small and brown, with large breasts that fell into his E-sensitised hands like pieces of heaven. She came loudly, twice.

See? he thought, satisfied, imagining her in the room beside them, awake, listening, crying.

He was afraid to wank in case she'd hear.

She woke religiously at the same time every morning. Seven. On the odd day Neil was awake then too, he'd hear her get out of bed. Then it would start. The heavy breathing from behind the black curtain. Ee-aw-ee-aw. He imagined her masturbating, lying on the sanded floor, legs open, pressing that tired fleshless button of hers, willing something to happen. Ee-aw. For twenty minutes, then she'd scoot up and race down to the shower as if frightened he'd get there first.

One night she came in pissed from an opening and forgot to pull the curtain over properly. The next morning he woke, too early, burning with the beginnings of a flu, unable to get back to sleep. From next door he could hear the breathing. Ee-aw. Harsh, fast, slow, fast. He couldn't stand it anymore, lying there, listening, that gap in the curtain calling to him like a friend, so he crawled down his bed and peeked through.

She was doing push-ups, naked. Her muscled back shone blue and orange in the early morning streetlamps. Her tiny buttocks clenched together. Her shaven head raised, lowered, raised. Downy hairs lifted up all over her skin. The tendons of her arms stood out like the knobbled bits on an Aran jumper. Her breath was harsh and fast.

Poor bitch, he thought, surprising himself with his pity.

He usually went out on Sundays but that week his parents were down the country, denying him roast dinner and the use of their washing machine. The sweetie from the café had gone back to Barcelona and his mates

32

were all split up; canoeing holiday, business conference and an open-air festival which he couldn't afford.

She was going out.

"There's this old market in the centre," she explained as he drank his coffee. "I want to capture it before they tear it down and turn it into another fucking pub for tourists."

"Tourists?" said Neil, slyly.

"And fuck you." She stubbed out her cigarette and, before he could say *Oh but I have* – "D'you want to come along?"

"Okay," he said, surprising himself again. "Why not?"

They headed off at three. Town was busy but the crowds thinned out as they got closer to the market. Rats deserting a sinking ship, lice fleeing a comb.

Neil helped her carry her cameras. She'd brought all three of them. One standard 35mm, one digital video – a present from "back home" – and one square brown box Neil didn't recognise. "Large-format," she explained. "Takes incredible pictures, really candid."

"Okay," she said, "here," and set the tripod down.

The building was large, glass-roofed, littered with old pallets and fruit papers. Oranges rolled in corners, bruised and oozing rancid juice. Scraps of tattered cloth dangled from the peak of the roof. Ancient signs, painted with the names of fruit & veg families who'd been there for centuries, hung overhead.

It was cold.

"There was a church here once," she said. "Underneath."

Neil thought of dark ecclesiastical passageways and black arched windows.

"They say people are buried there."

"People?"

"Yeah."

She began taking pictures. She was deliberate in her work, he saw. She would stand for minutes, looking, looking, smelling almost more than seeing, then move, decisive but not rushing, to the place where she

33

wanted to work, line up her camera, look through the lens, wait again – for ages it seemed to him, afterwards he thought it must have been to get the light right – then click. The click was over so quickly, compared to the waiting.

Jesus, he thought. *If only she could fuck the way she worked.*

It grew darker.

"Shouldn't we go?" he said. "I mean, the light – "

She shook her head. "No. This is the best time. Things come out of the walls at this time of day."

Left with no choice, he had to keep watching. Look, wait, smell, listen, bend, look, move the camera forward a bit, up a bit. She touched the camera with small gentle movements, as if it was a little child she was training to walk. It responded. They were dancing together, he realised. She and the camera, dancing in the dark.

As he observed her, he became calm. Her stillness leaked into him like pus.

"Why don't we explore?" he asked. The pictures were on the verge of being finished, he could tell that – by the way her head was inclining, perhaps, by a restlessness starting to itch itself into her right foot. He could tell she was about to finish and he didn't want her to. Anything would do, anything to keep things as they were.

"Oh," she said, surprised, looking around. "I was about to – "

"Yeah," he said. "But why not – I mean – you never know what we might find."

"Sure," she said. Half-smiling. A small puzzled frown on her forehead.

They found the door in a corner of the market, hidden behind a metal trolley laden with pallets and empty fruit boxes. It was not as he'd imagined it, oak and gothic, but square, dull-grey, sheet metal.

Someone had been there before them. One edge of the door was twisted up and away, jimmied with a knife or chisel. He stuck his fingers into the gap and pulled. The door screamed, metal against metal and opened a fraction. It was too small a gap for him to get through. He slid in his arm.

34

"Chancing your arm," she said. "Like the Normans."

"What?"

"That's where the saying comes from. The Normans used to stick their sword arms through this eentsy hole in the door so they could, you know, break through."

"Yeah?" he said. He couldn't budge it.

"Hey," she said. "Let me."

"You won't," he said, looking at the gap between the edge of the door and the wall.

"Trust me."

She turned herself sideways and edged her knee into the impossible gap.

Her shoulder disappeared, then her hip. Half of her body was on the other side of the door. She made a small, sighing sound and manoeuvred her other hip through.

"Ugh. Tight."

"Yeah," he said, feeling darkness creep up behind him.

"Okay! Head."

She squeezed her head backwards through the gap. It made him nauseous, thinking of the fragile bones in her skull, weakened by stewed fruit and too many push-ups, turn liquid under the pressure of metal and stone.

The tendons on her neck stood out, parallel lines, vulnerable. He wanted to touch them, stroke them like you would a baby's face. She melted into nothing.

"Okay," she said. From the other side, her voice was echoing and dark. "I'm gonna push."

You can't, he thought. Then remembered her daily grind of push-ups, the muscles on her body standing up like knitted blackberry stitch, and thought *Maybe you can.*

She pushed. The door screamed and shuddered.

Come on, come on, he thought, not wanting to be stuck in the darkening empty market like some forlorn ghost. The door screamed again.

"Grab it!" Her voice was muffled.

He seized the edge of the door and pulled. From the other side he felt the force of her body push; so much force for such a small body.

"Okay!" he called "Coming through!"

The pencil beam of her maglight shone on crumbling stone walls, moss, blackened rock, a few half-broken steps.

"Be Prepared," said Neil, indicating the light.

She ignored him.

At the bottom of the stairs was a second door. Much more like it. Panelled wood with iron clasps, set into a gothic arch. It had been pulled well off its hinges and swung open without a bother.

Inside, it was cold and damp, the floor slippery underfoot. Fungus glowed in the corners. The maglight flickered on ruined benches, pieces of old rotten wood, pews missing backrests and feet, crumbling arched recesses where holy pictures had once stood. At the top, what must have been the altar; a raised bank of stone speckled with lichen, covered with beer cans and cigarettes.

Neil laughed. "Jesus. I thought it was just a story."

"SShh!" she said, finger on her lips

Fucksake, he thought, *It's not a museum.*

At the back of the altar was a raised wooden casket. One of the doors hung loose on its hinge, the other was fastened tight. She walked up to it.

"Hey," he said, wanting to warn her but not sure why.

She ignored him and using one finger, swung the closed half-door open.

"Oh fuck!" she said, stepping back. Her torch clattered onto the ground, sending shadows racing over the walls. The maglight snapped off. They were in blackness.

"Oh Jesus!" She began to heave dry retches.

"Jule?" said Neil, on instinct calling her name, the way you'd call a hurt dog.

She started crying...

"It's okay," said Neil. "It's okay." He couldn't see where she was but moved towards the sound of her retching, her sobbing.

"It's okay. I'm here," he said. His outstretched hands came in contact with warmth, cheekbones, wet face.

He closed his arms around her. She crumpled into him, still sobbing.

"Okay," he said. "Ssssh. It's okay."

He kissed her forehead. She pressed into him, sniffling. His hands stroked her goosepimpled arms, the hairs that stood up on end, smoothing all into place. Behind her, as his eyes adjusted to the darkness, he saw something white gleam against the blackness of the altar.

"Easy," he said. This time she listened.

"They were bones," she told him as they walked home hand in hand through Dublin's deepening blue evening. "Children's bones. I could see their little faces and legs and –"

"It's okay," he said and squeezed her hand. She squeezed back, fingers thin thin thin like river reeds, autumn twigs.

The Last Elf-Mite

Jason Bellipanni

The elf-mites were quite adept at latching themselves onto words as they left the man's mouth. They had undergone extensive training and carried specialized mechanical sanders and saws. The instant the man's words had been set upon the air, these elf-mites stuck to them like lint, worked on each one with professional attention. The elf-mites shined the grooved teeth marks into seamless curvature, hammered the blunt protrusions into harmless nubs. They ground the man's rough words into softer, less abrasive morsels.

This group of elf-mites had been dispatched to this extremely distant outpost on an assignment to work for the woman, the boy, and the girl in the house. Upon arrival these skilled elf-mites immediately divided into companies and fell into a rigorous routine. For weeks they toiled in the house with the discipline of soldiers. They sweated profusely and often skipped meals without the slightest concern for their own well being, their own health. They were committed to perfection.

They expertly shaped "What the hell are you babbling about?" into "Excuse me, I believe I missed that."

They completely transformed "You're an idiot," and presented "Now I see your point of view."

Some elf-mites learned to ride the words like horses while they scrubbed furiously with ever-thinning squares of sandpaper. Others clung to the sides of the words like mountain climbers and melted the syllabic steel spikes with tiny gas torches. They learned to mold sound into beautiful figurines and flatten the harsh intonations like rolled pavement over a bed of jagged rocks.

As time went on the workload began to increase. Frustrated by the fact that he was unable to accurately express himself, the man began speaking at a relentless pace. He fired severe tonal buckshot and sharply angled words without pause, sent them spinning through the air like razor-sharp Chinese stars. The elf-mites needed a ground-breaking innovation or an evolutionary step that would help them adapt to the quickening pace, the increasing potency.

"You disgust me."

The miracle occurred one day on the woman's frontline. A particular elf-mite struggled, channeling all of his energy into polishing a particularly grotesque and dangerous deformity. His red face trembled as the sandpaper moved over the sharp metal claws, and sweat poured from the elf-mite like a shower. The black hole approached out of his peripheral vision.

If he did not abandon the broken word soon, he would be pulled into the infamous dark void where capture and agonizing death awaited him. It was said that the unlucky elf-mite who slipped into the black hole would be tortured into denying his own existence by the cruel army of reason. The guards of the military council of logic patrolled the porthole. No elf-mite had ever returned from the black hole.

Sucking every last molecule of energy from within, this brave elf-mite scrubbed furiously and bled onto the razor-sharp word as clouds of dust rose into his face, up his nose. The rich black hole grew larger beside him, tugged at him as he entered its gravitational field.

Firmly secured to his word and unwilling to abandon his project, this elf-mite screamed in defiance. His body exploded. The word was blasted out of existence and the incoherent bits spun away in every direction.

Elf-mites on the front lines throughout the house stopped for an instant to absorb what had just happened.

"I'm supposed to eat this – ?"

Another suicide explosion quickly followed the first, spreading the mist from a different word into oblivion. The woman heard the man's incomplete statements, the silent gaps in-between his phrases, and she asked him if he might be losing his voice.

The suicide technique was quickly studied by the elf-mites, refined into a simple process, and then taught in re-training sessions. At a moment's notice any elf-mite could now combust while attached to a word. This discovery temporarily helped ease the increasing workload since it took much less time to bomb away the key words than it took to completely sculpt phrases. The results were no longer as eloquent of course, but the elf-mites knew that protection came first and artistry only if time permitted.

The explosion process became extremely popular and the elf-mites moved ahead uninterrupted with their work. The day arrived, however, when the elf-mites suddenly realized that they had made a grave miscalculation in their haste to adopt the new suicide technique. The elf-mite population was plummeting and they were the only group dispatched to the area. They might never receive reinforcements, and most certainly not in time to avoid the imminent shortage.

The elf-mites shifted into super-overdrive in an attempt to maintain their schedule. They worked overtime, went without nourishment or rest for days, and they still could not keep up. Many of the young elf-mites were eager to become exploding white sparks, tiny puffs of honorable smoke, while many of the elders began to fall ill because of the increasingly hazardous working conditions. These elders could barely contribute to the various projects without fainting on their assigned words and diverting valuable elf-mite energy to their rescue.

Something had to be done and the solution, it turned out, required more courage and resolve from the elf-mites than they had ever given in the past.

They decided to abandon the woman. By re-calling elf-mites from that front, they would then have a sufficient number to continue covering the boy and the girl. On the day they withdrew from the woman, they felt a chill against their backs.

"Can you possibly be that stupid?!"

The elf-mites looked over their shoulder and saw the woman's mouth open, her eyes widen with shock. She absent-mindedly brushed her long black hair against her chest and remained silent. The man shook papers at the woman.

"Learn how to read!"

The elf-mites turned away and joined the others. They re-grouped, counted off, divided themselves into new units, and set out to work exclusively for the boy and the girl. The decision had been made and the elf-mites focused their energies on fulfilling their re-assigned duties.

Initially it was not easy to watch the woman crumble. She grew increasingly skittish and nervous. Her black hair turned mostly gray in a matter of weeks, and she had taken up the habit of constantly cleaning whenever the man was in the house. Just before the family sat down to dinner, the woman stood in the corner of the kitchen and pushed handfuls of potato chips into her mouth. She never touched the food on her plate.

The man tasted too much salt.

The woman made a comment about salt.

"Why do you open your mouth when you have no idea what you're talking about?"

On more than one occasion the elf-mites watched the woman take a word in the stomach like a bullet. She lost her breath for a moment, and then agreed, gave in, obeyed, or promised, whatever it took to stop the man from speaking. She gradually learned to submit without resistance, as if immediate surrender might calm the air, her blood and nerves. Unfortunately, she never evolved from the most primitive defense strategy. She continued to move constantly, her face twitched, her eyes squinted, as if she might be able to dodge the lightning cracks of the man's words and crawl to safety beneath the live-fire.

When the woman began to fade and flicker, the elf-mites experienced their next crisis. The woman washed the brick fireplace with a wet sponge and hummed to herself. Quite suddenly, the image of her wearing a faded yellow robe and matching bandana flickered like bad reception. For a moment, pure static filled her human form and this new creature knelt on the ground to rub invisible dirt with her thumb. After the woman was restored, she looked generally faded and one step closer to becoming a hologram.

It would probably not end well for the woman, the elf-mites knew. If she were lucky she would simply disappear one day, dissolve into streams of light, and speed past the elf-mites into the possibilities of the universe. They could only hope for the best.

The elf-mite population had once again fallen to dangerously low levels. They were only barely able to keep up and provide the boy and the girl with protection. Whole words began to slip through unaltered, even with the elf-mites hurling their bodies onto them, detonating them into oblivion.

"Cut it," he said to the girl. "You're less ugly with short hair, less fat."

The girl rose from the dinner table, tucking her brown hair behind one ear. She walked upstairs to the bathroom, closed the door, and turned on the sink faucet. The girl dropped to her knees and threw up in the toilet.

"Watch It eat," the man said sarcastically, looking at the boy. "Can It even stop to breathe?"

The boy and girl fronts had grown miserably thin and exhausted. Weary elf-mites watched their failures zip by without the will to make a dent, let alone sacrifice themselves.

They had to cut the boy loose. All they could hope to do now was preserve the girl for as long as possible. She was clearly the weakest, the most fragile. The elf-mites believed that the man's words would actually snap her in half, shatter her thin bones into her bloodstream. The elf-mites withdrew from the boy under the cover of darkness.

The elf-mites were renewed for a short period of time with a sense of duty, of purpose and hope. They gathered all of their remaining equipment together, re-stocked their packs and belts, counted off with strong voices, and fell in line. They would save the girl.

At night, the man stood over the girl lying in bed with his arms crossed against his chest. With her body beneath the blue blanket, she closed her eyes, and heard the man say, "Daddy loves you." The elf-mites erupted in a cheer, danced in the air, and slapped one another on the back.

The boy handled the elf-mite abandonment as well as could be expected. He withdrew into himself and puffed up his outer shell to absorb the man's words, as if his skin were a bulletproof vest. The boy installed locks on the inside of his bedroom door, and he sat on the top bunk squeezing coffee cake in his fist and shoving the pastry ball into his mouth. He wedged a fan in the window and the soothing noise put him to sleep at night, successfully scattering the sound from the rest of the house into unrecognizable bits around his room.

The woman floated through the house like a ghost, always moving, getting thinner and grayer by the hour. If she were unlucky the elf-mites knew that the woman would end in spectacular tragedy. A huddled mess, she would stutter and dodge and trip her way into a local pawnshop, constantly glancing over her shoulder. With eyes like a spooked horse she would point her trembling finger at the handgun inside the glass case and jerk her chin in an upward spasm; her request for the box of bullets stacked on an upper shelf.

The woman's muscles would suddenly relax, and she would stand tall. In one fluid motion the woman would pick up the gun, step back from the counter, slip a bullet into the chamber, and aim at her right temple. Before a word could be uttered in the pawnshop, the woman would fire the bullet into her head.

And though it would take some time, the elf-mites knew that the boy would eventually follow the path currently being cleared by the woman.

The girl, however, would not survive a single day on her own. Her body and mind had weakened as she watched the woman and boy slip away from her. They buckled and cowered under some invisible pressure, and they pushed the girl away when she asked them why. In her mind the man was her only hope, and if the elf-mites ceased activity, one word from him would certainly split the girl in half.

Meanwhile the situation became grave as the elf-mites continued to combust or otherwise disappear out of existence. Some simply broke into pieces from the persistent stress of their labor, the anguish caused by their increasing failures, while others calmly set the trigger and sacrificed themselves. Either way, they continued to pop into sparks and their numbers dwindled fast.

"You're as stupid as your mother."

The woman cleaned the brown heating vents on her knees with a toothbrush.

The man had finally beaten the elf-mites. Many of the most dependable and talented elf-mites would not surrender and so they suffered severe heart attacks while still attached to their words. Their lifeless bodies floated calmly into the black hole.

The girl was quietly left alone one morning, to be battered and bruised by the man's words in their roughest and rawest form, tumbling freely through the air like jagged chunks of gold ore.

43

Soon after the girl had been abandoned, the boy began to hear a voice in his head, but it was not a bad voice. It was a warm sound, coaxing and smooth. The pleasant voice gave him certain instructions and demanded that he tell no one or else the voice would vanish and never return. The boy quickly attached himself to the gentle voice and promised to please the voice in any way possible. The boy would have done anything to hear the comforting sounds of his only friend.

One night the boy broke through the window of a neighbor's vacant house and took a gun, which he unloaded, a stack of cash from an underwear drawer, and two tents from the basement.

The next day he brought the girl downtown to the bank and they each withdrew all of their childhood savings. The girl now kept herself together by wearing a yellow blanket tight around her shoulders, the two frayed corners crumpled inside her tiny fist. They walked across the street from the bank and the boy bought two long distance bus tickets for the next day. The children returned to the house.

It was a dangerous place to be for an elf-mite. Placed precariously at the entrance to the black hole, where even the slightest breeze could affect his balance, send him off the edge. Still, being the last elf-mite came with the greatest responsibility. He had suffered greatly in the struggles, being transferred from the woman to the boy and then to the girl. A true veteran. It took supreme concentration for this elf-mite to sit and cling to his place while he carved words and delivered them to the boy, directed his actions. The effort exhausted the elf-mite and he slept more and more throughout the day.

The boy and girl rose before sunrise on the next day. They dressed in the dark, gathered their pre-packed bags together, and took a jar of peanut butter and a loaf of bread from the cupboard. They made their way on tiptoe through the quiet house and opened the front door. The boy and girl stood next to each other on the front porch and took inventory of their supplies when they suddenly heard the woman clear her throat from the doorway behind them.

With their backpacks in place, duffel bags zipped and gripped in their hands, the two were prepared for the walk to the bus station.

The elf-mite struggled to stand and faced the dreaded moment with all of his strength. The woman could barely be seen by now, and she stood like an old movie image, flickering in the doorway, holding a toilet brush in one hand. The elf-mite took in as much air as possible and summoned every bit of energy that remained in his being. He crouched in place and waited.

The woman shook her head, a solitary figure standing like a ghost in front of the silent dark living room. She did not appear angry or surprised, but she shook her gray head with sadness. It was too late for her.

Fear rose like a beast from deep inside the woman and seized control of her body, tightened her stringy muscles. She gripped the toilet brush like a club and stared hard at the boy. The woman made one last attempt to avoid her fate, to pull that destined bullet back through her temple and into the cold harmless gun. Two words to try and suck the two children into her void and fill her with warmth against the spreading bone chill of loneliness. The woman opened her mouth to speak.

When the pleading words, "Don't go," left the woman's mouth, the last elf-mite heaved into action. He concentrated every bit of strength into one final jump, and leapt from his post to land with expert poise on the crucial traveling word. He could feel the black hole approaching from behind at an impossible rate of speed.

The last elf-mite held tight, closed his eyes, and ignited himself from within. In a single blink of the boy's eye, the last elf-mite successfully blasted the word "Don't" into a fine, silent mist.

Tow

Morgan McDermott

It took five years for Bruni to learn the trick to mastering a blind dog. It took that long for her to understand the nuances of discipline, to realize that to officer is at once to love, and to limit. She has learned that it is essential to never let a blind dog lose sight of who is leading whom; a blind dog, after all, cannot read halfhearted gestures or mixed signals. Failing to train a blind dog properly is in itself an act of cruelty. After five long years of learning that to love anything, or anyone, is to be George S. Patton at times, Bruni is confident she now has the skills to take on a young man.

The young man leans his shoulder casually against the bulletproof window in the tow office. He unwraps a stick of chewing gum thoughtfully, pondering his next words, as they may make or break him in the eyes of his girl. This is how the young man thinks of their courtship. He thinks of it as a horse race. He thinks that how he exits the gate means everything.

The tow office is an aluminum trailer with curved, reflective interior walls. A posting from the police is bolted into the metal, as official as the Ten Commandments. The curve creates a fun-house mirror effect, capturing those who enter, twisting them into freaks. There is nowhere in the shiny room that those who have come for their cars might sit, so Bruni stands against the wall by the door. The surface hurts her elbows, but she does not let it show on her face. She has been practicing not showing pain. Living with a sighted person soon, she will have to speak a whole new body language.

The young man chews three sticks of gum at once. It lends him the air of a wrangler, a bull-rider, a man who knows how to wrestle trouble with his hands. It is early in their relationship. She is still convincing him that she finds him handsome, and manly, and smart. He is still learning how to champion her. He is still learning which problems she wants him to solve, and which ones she only needs to talk about. He has decided this moment falls into the first category.

The young man leans close to the glass and asks Mr. Tow if Mrs. Tow is happy married to a hijacker. Mr. Tow shakes his head sadly, explaining this detail for perhaps the thousandth time. Through the circular metal speaker in the center of the window, Mr. Tow says that there is no Mrs. Tow, and in fact there is no *Mr. Tow*: the name is franchised, a corporate logo. Then he says if the young man wants the car, he must pay for the tow and the hourly storage like everyone else. Mr. Tow points to the sign above the window.

ALL VIOLATORS ARE EQUAL IN THE EYES OF MR. TOW the sign reads.

Bruni and the young man need the car to start their new life together. The car is roomy, an SUV with leather seats and a tow bar mounted below the bumper. They need it to carry Bruni's belongings from her apartment to what will be their apartment, once one is found. Bruni desperately needs it so they can move into a mutual space at the same time. She does not want to suffer the stigma of the space being *his* first, and only later one shared. She wants them to start this adventure on an equal footing, as equal partners.

That equality is now in doubt. This afternoon they were treated to the chilling sight of a vanished automobile. The street where they had left it had been swept clean of parked cars. Bruni knew at once that she now would not be allowed to use the car, that any footing she might have had in argument with her sister, any claim to adult privilege, had been towed away. She knew at once that her escape, perhaps even her courtship, was in trouble.

The young man asks if Mrs. Tow is proud that he is a pirate, that he chose privateering as a career.

Bruni checks her watch. Five minutes, and counting. The young man promised her that he could reason with Mr. Tow and have the SUV back in ten. She looks down at the newspaper she holds folded to the want ads: luxury townhouses are available next to the university campus, two

47

and three bedrooms. Astronomical rent. She continues down the page.

Mr. Tow says his *wife* is proud that he runs a successful business, and thanks the young man for asking.

Her sister pokes Bruni in the shoulder, the poke she has when she has a question. Brynne has just entered the trailer from the parking lot, where she has let her blind dog off the leash to roam. She has missed most of the action. Whispering, she asks if Mr. Tow is tall. Bruni says the man is tall, yes, but not attractive. She says Mr. Tow is Abe Lincoln-tall. Brynne likes only tall men, and though she is blind, she usually does not have to ask. The speaker, and the curved walls, and the fact that Bruni is leaving her, are all throwing off her perception.

Mr. Tow says if the young man mentions his wife again, there will be trouble. He calls the young man Buster.

Brynne and her blind dog are present because they own the SUV. When people ask why a blind woman owns a car – and a car the size of Panama at that – Brynne claims she bought it for the dog. The chocolate lab was in the seeing-eye business, and is frustrated in its retirement. She tells everyone that hearing the dog bump into the furniture pains her, and that long rides with the windows open would be a tonic. It would be a safe way for the dog to enjoy itself.

Bruni knows the real reason. The real reason is that Bruni's driving makes Brynne nervous. Brynne never liked being driven by her little sister, even before the accident, and now she wants an island of steel around her as a buffer. Five years of living with Brynne has taught Bruni that buffers, whether constructed out of steel, or bulletproof glass, or sharp words, not only protect, they keep others in step.

Mr. Tow tells the young man to grow up, that there is nothing personal in having a car towed. Mr. Tow says some people choose to believe only they can move their cars. They are fools.

At the auto dealership, Brynne told the salesman she had nearly died in a traffic accident, and insisted on only looking at the largest SUVs in stock. Bruni recalls how her sister selected the model by touching the machine front to back, measuring inside and out, rapping the sheet metal to gauge its ability to absorb a hit. The salesman grew excited when Brynne did not bother to look at the brochures. He was in the passenger seat for the test drive before he realized she was blind. Bruni remembers the look of deliberation on the man's face as he considered handing her the keys anyway, as he wrestled with the benefits versus the risks.

Brynne is an object of deliberation for many men. They weigh carefully her pros and cons, weigh the effort required to be with her against the softness of her golden hair, the smoothness of her skin, the timbre of her voice. Perhaps she does not have sight, but she has looks, and Bruni knows women who would think long and hard about that trade. The men who decide to court Brynne take her to the movies, where they love whispering details into her perfect ears. They take her to art galleries so she can breathe in the masters. Eventually these men grow comfortable enough to take her to dinner just so they can look into her luminous, decorative brown eyes and admire themselves without reservation. It is about that point when Brynne dumps them.

Bruni remembers how the salesman clenched his hand slowly around the keys, how he kept them hidden until Bruni stepped forward and offered to drive. She remembers how the salesman smiled as though he had won a hand of poker. Left to make the car-buying decision herself, Bruni would have told the salesman to tell his story walking. She would have kept the old Honda, its bodywork long ago hammered back into shape, its windshield replaced. She would have saved the cash and put the dog to sleep. But that would have sent the wrong message to her sister.

The young man kicks the wall gently as he speaks. He says if there is nothing personal, if no one should take offense, then why does Mr. Tow hide behind a bulletproof shield?

Mr. Tow eyes Brynne as the young man speaks. He eyes her legs. Mr. Tow gives Bruni the impression of a man who drinks most of his meals. He has the long face, the sad eyes, the pouty lips of a man who trained to climb a professional ladder but lost his footing and slid several rungs before halting. He looks like he is holding on too tightly to that ladder to drop any further, but also too tightly to pull himself up. Mr. Tow must know his is not a good look for a man in his post. Eyes on Brynne, Mr. Tow straightens up, thrusts his chest forward, squares his shoulders.

Bruni snorts. She gets a kick out of the preening men do around her blind sister, the adjusting of ties, the running of hands through hair, the discreet removal of wedding rings.

The young man says since Mr. Tow is in the ransom business, he should at least look the part: he should wear a vest, a hoop earring, a cloth around his head. He should wear an eye patch.

Mr. Tow says it is all funny until someone loses an eye.

Brynne grinds her teeth. Even at a distance, Bruni hears the jaw muscles click. It sounds like a coin striking pavement, calling for attention.

The young man says he is surprised anyone finds Mr. Tow funny. He is a man who steals for a living. He is a man who inflicts trauma.

Mr. Tow says he steals nothing. The cars go home eventually.

The young man asks about the mountains of cars stacked outside in the wrecking yard.

Mr. Tow says those cars are not displaced, they are disloved. He says all the cars that end up at his establishment suffer from some degree of dislove, from a lack of attention to detail that only comes from weariness with love, the wish that what was once an object of adoration would just go away already.

Bruni presses herself against the wall. She assumes the room was designed narrow to avoid mob action. With her and the young man and Brynne, the air is tight, and it puts her in mind of a tomb. The narrow trailer sits on a gravel lot stacked high with automobile carcasses, stacks that remind Bruni of Egypt, of the Sphinx and the pyramids. Bruni has not been to Egypt. Bruni has been nowhere, but she has cable television. Every time she suggests travel to Brynne, she meets resistance. When Bruni suggests they drive the SUV up to Montreal, or down to Memphis, her sister says she does not want to risk it. The way Brynne says *risk*, Bruni hears clearly the shriek of rubber on pavement, the crunch of glass as the crown of Brynne's head breaks the windshield. It has taken five years for Bruni to admit there is living without sight, and then there is living without vision, and that her poor driving inflicted only one of these conditions on her sister.

The young man tells Mr. Tow that love is not the issue in this case. He says the issue is his car was towed without fair warning. Tilting his head, catching the discrepancy, Mr. Tow says that when he first came to the window, the young man stated it was not *his* car that was towed, but a friend's. Mr. Tow's voice is stern. He is the victim of a lie.

Brynne startles them both when she interrupts, when she says that they are wasting her time. She steps forward and says the car does not belong to a friend of the young man, it belongs to her. She says she is not the young man's friend. He has stolen her sister's heart, and he is without a substantial job, and he borrows her car without asking.

Mr. Tow says it is the young man who should wear an eye patch.

The young man says it is a long story.

Mr. Tow says that he can see on Brynne's face, and on the young man's face, and on the face of the girl standing by the door holding the want ads, much of that story. He says the young man should invest in some bulletproof glass, as it helps everything appear more manageable.

As she listens to the men, Brynne's head moves as though spectating a tennis match.

She is a professional listener. She handles collection calls for the state child-support agency. The calls come to the apartment on a dedicated line, and between eight and four Chicago time Brynne confronts deception and insult and hard-luck stories. She reads silence the way a sighted person reads facial muscles. She reads a good lie like an oenophile reads a fine wine, reveling in the hints and blush of its heritage, appreciating the skill behind its crafting. She fits what a man tells her together with what he does not like puzzle pieces, assembling a complete picture of both the problem and the man.

When Brynne is on the job, she will sometimes put her party on hold and describe to Bruni what the deadbeat is wearing. Brynne can tell a deadbeat's age to the year, and where he or she was born. She can tell if a deadbeat is rich or poor; fat or thin. She can tell who is healthy, and who is headed for the pine-box derby. While they are dating, some men assume Brynne has ESP. When they are discharged, many accuse her of being a witch. Bruni is not bothered by her sister's talent. She enjoys the details of people far away. It is a little like traveling.

Brynne turns to Bruni and says that the young man is going about this all wrong, that he does not *listen*. She says Bruni will be able to do nothing with this young man. She speaks loudly enough for the young man to hear.

Bruni concentrates on her reading: one bedroom, one bath, but in a high-rise building, with a pool and a heated garage, boosting the monthly well out of reach. She does not circle the phone number. Brynne presses on, says there is not one bit of *give* in the young man, that he will be dead of burst pipes and disappointment at a young age. She says Bruni has much to learn about disappointment in men. She says that it is like rust on a car. Disappointment eats away at a man.

Bruni fixes her eyes on the newspaper because she cannot look anywhere else without meeting a twisted face. She fixes on an ad for a three bedroom, one bath coachhouse, all utilities included. Just the word *coachhouse* makes her shiver, the thought of living behind a lakefront house, living servant-class, under scrutiny. Living small.

Bruni has served the last five years under careful watch, learning that being visually able is not the same thing as being visible. She has learned her lesson. After the accident, she skipped going away to college. She lived with Brynne in the condominium bought with the insurance settlement and took classes at the local school. She was of use. She had been a precocious child, in possession of the precocious child's distaste with being young. She is over that now.

Brynne says Bruni does not have to listen. It is enough for now that she just hears.

Bruni tries hard to hear elsewhere. Outside, other tow victims stand on the gravel path to the trailer, waiting patiently to be fleeced. They are all neighbors, made criminals by arcane street-cleaning tow zones that appear and disappear with the seasons. Focusing on their conversations, Bruni is not surprised by the lack of grumbling. In this college town just north of the city, very professional, very educated people routinely toe illogical lines without complaint. Residents are accustomed to being soaked by taxes and fines and tickets. The civic abuse is the price they endure for the privilege of living along the lake. Bruni is not surprised by the festive air: business cards are exchanged, mutual friends are discovered, the names and telephone numbers of good baby-sitters float for all to hear. Those waiting in line were rattled when their heaviest, most expensive, most *trusted* belonging was snatched up by the undertow of

52

civilization. They have lived in the wrong time and place for at least a moment. They have had a taste of Czarist Russia, or Oklahoma in the spring. They are relieved to be reminded that they are all Americans, and that to right their world requires only a credit card.

Bruni lets the tow victims' chatter flow over her like music as she scans the columns of print: one bedroom, one bath, near the lake, the rent a nice punch in the mouth. She marks it anyway, to bolster her resolve. She will look at it. She might not be able to afford many of the listings, but she also cannot afford to stay where she is.

The young man asks Mr. Tow to be reasonable. It is midsummer. There is no snow to plow. The SUV was parked neither in front of a hydrant, nor in a bus zone. No crime took place. Why must people suffer?

Mr. Tow says he takes no action out of cruelty; signs clearly command one not to leave a car where it does not belong, and when that commandment is broken, he appears.

The young man says that what happened to him is not fair. He says Mr. Tow should see where some people park: in front of hydrants, in handicapped spots, on sidewalks. *Sidewalks*. He says those are real sins. Mr. Tow agrees free will is often abused, but says he always catches up in the end.

The young man says Mr. Tow is wrong to claim he is not cruel.

Mr. Tow says he would not say it if he did not believe it.

Mr. Tow is saved by the bell, the cheerful *ting* of a microwave from the rear of the office. Mr. Tow turns, and is gone. The young man faces an empty window.

Brynne's head tilts as she tracks the sound of Mr. Tow's footsteps. The tension washed from the room for the moment, the air quiet, Bruni's senses come out from under cover; she notices that the room smells doughy and damp, of cheap frozen pasta. Outside, the dog is playing with the crowd, growling as it offers its toy, a hard rubber ball with a rattle inside. One of the dog's favorite games since going blind is tug-of-war. It likes to assert its physical presence, exercise its ability to push, and to pull. The lab is still young. When it had sight, it was docile, but it has found fire in recent years, found mischief.

She peeks through the doorway and sees one of the tow truck drivers playing with the dog, twirling in a circle and forcing it to turn in dance-step with him as he tries to wrestle the ball from clenched jaws. The dog and the man match each other grunt for grunt, both of them accustomed to having say over direction. Short and thick, the driver wears threadbare gray overalls with a red and white patch over his breast pocket.

SOFOCLES, the patch reads.

The young man places his open palms on the glass, then a cheek, angling to see where his adversary went. Face to the glass, he tells the women that he has the tow guy on the ropes.

Brynne tells the young man to hush up.

Bruni looks from the young man, to her sister, to the advertisements. She pauses over a bold announcement: a vintage apartment, two bedrooms, two baths, located in an upscale neighborhood in the college town, renting for twice what she can afford.

Her pen hovers over the ad.

To earn money Bruni writes term papers on commission, twenty dollars a page. She writes papers on any subject, for she loves to learn. Her favorites are English and history, and currently she is writing a master's thesis on the mistakes that led to World War Two, the resentments and grudges. She is learning how the world can be torn apart when people refuse to let go of the past. Bruni figures that if she works another job, works retail or waits tables, she might be able to live a lifestyle advertised boldly.

The young man says the tow guy is buckling, that he almost has the car.

Brynne says this is a first for her, a man who knows nothing about women, and also knows nothing about men.

The young man's shirt is open at the collar, and as his skin flushes, as he reddens, Bruni catches sight of the scars at his neck, scars that trail like latticework down his chest. Her young man is a survivor. He has survived a shooting, and more importantly he has survived its healing, has avoided the cruel demeanor that can come from regarding oneself as a victim. She is still learning the scars by sight and by touch, still learning his landscape. Bruni lowers the newspaper and says they parked her sister's car poorly, she and the young man, and they can take responsibility. They can pay the fine. They might have acted poorly, but they are not poor.

Brynne says that if Bruni marries this man, she will have to clean up after him coming and going.

The young man tells Brynne to keep her mouth shut if she cannot see the big picture.

Bruni wants to kiss him. All her boyfriends have been partly in love with her older and stronger and more beautiful sister. Bruni knows that to be in love with such a woman is partly to be afraid of her. But this young man is not cowed by Brynne. This young man does not flinch.

Brynne says that the young man is miffed because he knows she has his number.

The young man says Brynne may have his number, but he has Bruni.

Brynne tells the young man that her sister will grow bored with him. She says that like Jean-Paul Sartre, her sister will always have an eye somewhere else.

As Brynne speaks, the young man steps away from the glass to stand at Bruni's side. He tries to put his arm around Bruni, but he comes too close and steps on her toes. Bruni is wearing sandals and the misstep hurts magnificently, but she does not show it. Her practice is paying off. To hide her grimace, she turns away, looks out the door. In the lot, the chocolate lab is toying with the crowd, walking away slowly enough to be pursued, ball in mouth, tail wagging in defiance. The driver stands with his hands on his hips, calling to the dog in Spanish. The animal continues toward the automobile graveyard. The driver claps his hands, trying to be sweet, to no effect. He knows none of the tricks.

Brynne advances on the spot where the young man stood just a moment before. She stands sideways to Mr. Tow's window. She faces the emptiness in such a way that an observer could not help but conclude she has made a mistake, that she thinks the young man stands before her still. Brynne faces her distorted reflection on the far wall and, next to it, the legal disclaimer posted by the police. Bruni has seen Brynne do this when denied her way. Bruni has seen her sister look high over the head of someone in order to put that person off balance, or let her head sway back and forth when she wants to shame an opponent into silence.

Speaking into thin air, Brynne accuses the young man of being so immature that he assumes to sleep with a woman is to know her. She warns the young man that he will regret carrying her sister away the minute he realizes how much of a woman is composed of secrets. She addresses the wall and its posted notice vehemently, her usual cool manner carefully, expertly disassembled.

YOU HAVE THE RIGHT TO AN APPEAL reads the notice.

Bruni feels the young man's grip fade around her, his resolve ebbing as he confronts a handicapped woman lost without her sister, literally not knowing which direction to turn. His hand falls to his side. Bruni takes hold of his arm, the same way she holds her sister when crossing a busy intersection.

Outside, several of those waiting their turn are whistling for the blind dog, calling to it, some calling it Girl, some calling it Boy.

The young man slips Bruni's grasp without a word, steps through the door into the lengthening shadows of the late afternoon. Bruni watches him stalk toward the flattened and stacked autos, the American pyramids, ancient ruins of the modern world. She knows he will fare no better than the truck driver. The dog will dodge him. It frustrates the young man that the dog does not listen. He assumes the dog does not listen because it does not like him. He has not yet learned the trick to commanding a blind dog is to earn its respect, to acquire its trust while breaking its will. Bruni is debating whether or not to teach him.

As soon as he is gone, Brynne turns to Bruni, facing her dead on.

You'll see, Brynne says.

Bruni returns to the newspaper: two bedrooms, one bath, hardwood floors and lots of light, but only a summer sublet, a temporary solution. Bruni writes a question mark next to the ad. There is a shuffling in the back of the office. The aroma of wet noodles has faded. Brynne turns to the window, gathers her hair behind her head, then lets it fall evenly, fan out over her shoulders. Brynne's nose sweeps the air, and Bruni realizes her sister has been following the steady disappearance of Mr. Tow's food, that she has been timing the moment the man's break will end, collecting herself for her presentation, marshaling her forces.

Brynne knows all the tricks.

Tinkerbell

Elizabeth Brinkley

Mary and I were driving out of the suffocating haze of Los Angeles into the dry, windy heat of the desert when she said, "I can't wait to see Tink." The ownership of a dog was something our small apartment made impossible, so we visited our friends Chiles and Eva about once a month, partly so Mary could visit Chiles's 98-pound rottweiler, Tinkerbell. We also went because, in the way that so many friendships between couples work, Mary liked Eva and I liked Chiles.

Eva had a cloying southern temper, cooked things like cupcakes and gingerbread cookies, as if for a school bake sale, and wore gauzy, shapeless dresses over her skeletal body, all of which I found intolerable. Somehow she had ended up with Chiles. Mary considered Chiles an arrogant, peevish druggie who ignored Eva and never looked for legitimate employment because it was too easy to live off Eva's trust fund. This was basically true, though Chiles contributed monetarily in his own illegal fashion. Chiles was an anomaly, lazy with what disinterested him yet full of a manic, contagious energy that attracted people to him like they were drawn to the pot or coke or heroin he sold.

Mary sat in the passenger seat, wearing a coral tank top she knew I liked, cleaning her sunglasses with its hem. She wasn't asking me not to get stoned as soon as we got there, so I knew she was really hoping we could be, for the weekend, a couple together instead of pairing off by gender every time we took this trip. After three years, these tacit negotiations had become as commonplace as sentences finished by the other person, and a long road trip shared mostly in silence was a testament to a thick and time-tested love rather than boredom or awkwardness.

I had known she would, in her adorable eagerness, mention Tinkerbell. Chiles had bought Tink off the Internet from a high-end breeder two years ago. He had trained him well, Chiles's discipline producing a gentle, responsive nature, and sometimes I think he loved that dog more than his girlfriend. Eva might have thought so too, if she were astute enough, which I doubted. Tink's cultivated personality should have proved Chiles's essential good-heartedness to Mary, but she passed it off as a fluke.

Later that afternoon, chicken and steak were marinating and coals smoldered on the grill. Inside the house, the air-conditioning was on high, and Chiles and I were very stoned. We sat on the couch, watching the girls outside through the sliding glass door. Chiles and Eva had a small orange grove in their backyard and I couldn't help laughing as I watched Eva, her long skirt brushing the uncut grass, clutching a handful of plastic bags, pick up dog shit and rotten oranges.

Mary was in the pool with Tink. Mary was a flexible, athletic swimmer. She was not exactly pretty, but cute, and she had a nice body. I took another hit and watched her treading water, holding the ball up high in the air, then throwing it for Tink, who lumbered out of the pool and splashed heavily back in for another round.

Chiles said, "Mary doesn't like me very much, does she?"

"No," I said, exhaling. "But she likes you enough."

Chiles took another hit, talking weakly through full lungs.

"Jimmy got busted in New Jersey. I lost twenty pounds of product."

This was shocking. I'd always thought of Chiles as a small timer, and suddenly one of his lackeys had gone down.

"Shit," I said. "Will he do time?"

"No doubt. I told him not to go through New Jersey. Of every fucking state in the union, you don't take drugs through New Jersey."

This was the sheetrock-hard Chiles, the slightly scary Chiles, and I ended the conversation with a grunt of put-on understanding and empathy. I didn't want to think about Jimmy, who had been at the house a couple of times, or the actual drug dealer Chiles, with all that meant: prison and AIDS and strung-out junkies moaning in withdrawal. I just wanted to get high and watch my girlfriend swim.

Chiles was staring at Mary in the pool. Eva had disappeared. Flames hovered above the empty grill.

I sat there thinking, *I love my girlfriend.*

Mary's always spilling things on herself, and I laugh at her every time and she laughs back. Her idea of making a bed is throwing the bedspread over tangled sheets in one swift motion, as if she were covering a dead person. When she talks about us, whether it's something uncomfortable or something pleasurable, she tilts her head up to the sky.

That's when it happened. Out at the pool. Mary and Tink were playing as usual, but Mary had held the ball above him a moment too long, I guess, an unintended tease. Tink cupped his jaws around Mary's neck and they sunk as one, the ball he sought to bring down still in her hand. As she went under, it rolled out of her fingers and bobbed on the wavy surface of the water.

I couldn't make my feet move, but Chiles was already shoving the glass door to the side. Mary and the dog came up, still attached, hair covering Mary's mouth as she opened it for breath before Tink hauled her down again. Fear and pot made me dizzy, and I hung on the door handle, watching Chiles dive in, and then they were all underneath.

When they rose, Chiles had one hand on the dog's wet leather collar and one hand partially down his throat, trying to break the grip. It worked. Mary fell back and reached haltingly for the side, where she rested her head and heaved.

It turned out the bite had been something like a bird dog's on a prize pheasant, and Mary only had some red dots on her neck. On the floor of the living room, where we were all gathered, I had my arm around her, and I could feel, through the wet towel Chiles had wrapped around her, her trembling subside. Eva asked about tea, as if Mary needed any more water in her throat, for chrissake. We were all winding down. Tink, oblivious, was sunning himself on the carpet, panting through one of those half-smiles that dogs make. There was talk of putting something on the grill.

Chiles had been silent this entire time. He sat on the hearth, dripping, flinging away some dry clothes Eva had brought for him. He went into the bedroom and came out with something in his hand. He yanked Tinkerbell up from his lying position, evoking a whimper.

Then we all saw what he was holding.

Mary was on him like a cat, her hand tiny against the thick one that held the gun, but Chiles only humiliated her, raising the pistol up out of her reach.

"You can't," she wailed.

Easily slipping out of Mary's arms, Chiles leashed Tink, who had recovered from the harsh awakening and whined excitedly, ready for some great adventure.

"Mary, get away from the gun," I said. "Please, come to me."

No response. Then Eva spoke to her boyfriend. "If you're going to do it, get out of here now. Into the orchard."

"Chiles, you're not going to do anything." I was slowly moving toward Mary, trying to get close enough to pull her away.

"Chiles, you're high," I said. "Eva, tell him to let Tink go and put the goddamn gun down."

Eva turned on me. "Why are you protecting that dog? He almost choked your girlfriend. I told Chiles, there's always a first time for these breeds. He wouldn't listen." She straightened up. "Now he has to do what needs to be done."

"You are such a bitch," I said.

Finally I could grab Mary from behind.

"Let go of me," she screamed, but I held her tight. This was the moment for her to turn and let me take her in my arms, but she wouldn't do it. She just kept struggling and begging Chiles not to shoot the dog.

"Chiles, put it down, now," I said.

He started to walk toward the door with Tink in one hand, the gun in the other.

"My dog could've killed you," he said to Mary, his voice breaking, and something about the way he looked at her made my stomach contract.

"If you kill Tink," she said, "it will always be because of me. You won't want to, but you'll start resenting me, then hating me." She sagged in my arms. "I couldn't bear it if you hated me."

Chiles stared back at her, his expression a mixture of fondness and reproach.

I looked to where the gun fell on the floor. There were four indentations from a chair, and black marks in a small cluster where some man, the previous owner, had sat alone, watching TV or gazing outside, letting his cigarettes fall and singe holes in the carpet, over and over.

I let go of Mary. For a few long seconds, no one moved.

I went into the other room to start packing, but my duffel was untouched, so I sat on the edge of the bed in the dark.

Mary had told me she'd been promoted, letting her travel more. This excuse was unoriginal for someone like Mary, but giving her new situation much thought might've taken the edge off her high. I think I'd said something like great, now we can get digital cable. It was a joke on my own jobless status, and she had laughed, her curls falling across her wide smile. Her laugh had relieved me, had let me think she still loved me despite my inability to obtain steady work, or even want it. Now I knew that the love I had felt then was just the reflected glow of her new infatuation. There was so much love to go around.

Mary came into the room, sobbing. She said nothing. I knew she was afraid to talk, was afraid of me now, and I gloated in it. She wouldn't stop crying. Her stupid tears seemed to demand something of me, something I wasn't even close to giving. I turned to her.

"If you're coming with me you better cut that shit out, pack your suitcase, and get in the fucking car."

She sucked in a breath and picked up her bag. Hands shaking, she stuffed in t-shirts, socks, her wet bathing suit. We walked out through an empty living room.

As I drove around the front of the house onto the street, we passed Eva, kicking up dust with each sluggish, bare-footed step. Her expression was blank, otherworldly. For a second I wanted to stop the car, get out, and put my arms around her. I would have felt the boyish edges of her thinness, and the fire of whatever was roiling inside of her. I would have let go and walked away without a word.

Instead, Mary and I drove back to LA together, in the stuffy thickness of sweat and chlorine and pain. Words wouldn't form in my head. I could feel only the ugly sensations of each passing moment. As for Mary, I had no idea what she might be thinking, and at the time, I didn't care. In those two hours, with both of us next to each other in our own worlds of hurt, a creeping, bitter loneliness shoved up against my love for Mary, which wouldn't give way. As we pierced through the darkness, every part of me ached with that battle.

The Visit

Freda Churches

Mammy and I travelled on the bus to Greenfields. She never walked anywhere if she could help it, especially if it was wet. Today she was wearing boots, and a jacket with a raincoat on top. She could hardly bend to sit down. She half-lay on the seat with her legs sticking out while I drew pictures on the windows and stared at the sky, so low it seemed to be sitting on the roof.

I don't see what's wrong with wearing a rainmate. She frowned at my dripping locks. Mark my words Lily, you're going to end up with double pneumonia.

She'd tied it tightly under her chin and pulled it into a beak at the front to protect her fringe. I could think of a million reasons why I didn't want to be seen with a piece of plastic on my head, but mammy would never understand. When it was time to get off, she stood up and waddled downstairs while I followed at a safe distance. You never knew who you might meet, even on a day like this, and I didn't want folk to know she belonged to me.

We lived on the corner of Northfield Avenue and Avon Street, mammy, dad and me, and Nana, who was half gypsy and ancient. In spite of her great age my grandmother's views on fashion and music were modern. In the evenings we'd lie on her bed and tune into Virgin Radio. They played all sorts, but we preferred the black singers because they sang in a way that made our hearts shiver.

Nana had gone to Greenfields for a while to give mammy 'a wee rest'. She'd started doing some funny things; spitting at people in the street and calling them peasants, taking her teeth out in cafés and using her mouth as a pea-shooter at mealtimes. Anything she didn't fancy was rolled into a glob and launched through the air at a tremendous rate. Food hadn't the same appeal to an old person, she explained. She'd been on this earth so long her tastebuds had worn dry.

The nursing home was a tall, sandstone building with lots of chimneys, narrow windows and a long gravel driveway at the front surrounded by railings. I had no idea why they called it Greenfields. Apart from a few withered shrubs, there was hardly a blade of grass in sight.

When we arrived, a care assistant informed us that Nana was in the smoking lounge, which was exactly as she described – a room full of smoke with some chairs around the walls, and a television in the corner. A few of the residents were peering through the haze at the screen. Everyone had their favourite chairs, except Nana. She didn't care where she sat and this often upset certain folk. Today was no exception. She'd chosen a small velvet couch over by the window and an old woman with pink curls was wandering around making faces and muttering to herself. I'd never seen anyone with pink hair before.

Hello Lottie, mammy placed a couple of stools next to Nana's feet. How are you today?

Ah'm keeping fine. Nana turned and smiled at me. Hello Lily. Her eyes travelled across my face. You're getting to look more like a young Elizabeth Taylor every day.

I hugged her, caught a whiff of Coty L'aimant and tobacco and felt something warm ripple through me. I'd missed her smell. That warm smoky scent that seemed to envelop her.

The woman with the pink curls was still circling the floor. Every so often she stopped and gave herself a slap.

Is she new? Mammy lowered her voice and nodded backwards. She was good at speaking with her lips closed.

Och, never mind her, Nana glared across the room. She's half-cracked. Have you brought any fags Grace?

Mammy dropped a packet in her lap and we sat down. The television was blaring. A man with a sad face was reading the news.

'Trouble is once again brewing in the Middle East.'

A film of some soldiers flashed onto the screen. They were loading their rifles and grinning. Suddenly, one of the men stepped forward with a machine gun and fired into the ground. The old woman who was going round and round jumped and gave herself another whack on the head. The soldiers were laughing and whooping behind clouds of dust. It was scary the way everybody was starting to fight.

So, tell me all your news. Nana looked at us.

Oh everything's fine, mammy smiled. Lily's working hard at the big school. And I've had plenty of overtime at the sweet factory. Which reminds me. I've brought you these. She unzipped her bag and handed Nana some broken fudge.

There's going to be another war, I said.

Ah hope it's no toffee. Nana rolled her gums together. It sticks to ma plate.

There's a war going on. Between Israel and Palestine, I pointed to the television. It's on the news.

Mammy glanced at the screen. Oh Lily, that's away in another country. It has nothing to do with us.

She lit two cigarettes and handed one to Nana. I wafted my hand about, and added a few coughs, but they kept on talking.

It's absolutely bucketing down outside. Mammy glanced out the window.

You're in the best place Lottie.

This was one of her favourite phrases. Whenever the weather was bad, or the sink got choked, or the water pipes froze. You're in the best place Lottie, she'd say. As if my grandmother was the luckiest person alive.

The Israeli airforce were taking off in huge jets. I hurried across and changed the channel. As long as you didn't switch it off no one seemed to mind which side they watched.

Don't be cheeky! Mammy grabbed my arm. You go right over and switch it back.

I flicked the knob again and sat down.

In the name of the wee man! Nana puffed on her cigarette. That's an awfy dour face for a young lassie to be wearing. Come and tell me what you've been getting up to Lily.

We chatted for a while about school and how much I enjoyed the biology class and I reminded her of how much I wanted to be a doctor one day and showed her a picture of a cancerous lung that I'd cut out of an old anatomy book.

Just then, one of the carers appeared with a tray of tea and biscuits.

How are you today auld yin? she asked, in a loud voice.

Her name was Janice Carruthers and I didn't like her. She called Nana auld yin, to make herself feel good. To remind everyone that she was still young.

She pressed the pink-haired woman into a seat by the door and handed out some cups. Old Macum Taylor, half asleep in the corner, poured some tea into the saucer and gave it a blow. He had a wart on his chin that went up and down as he spoke and trousers that seemed to grow from his armpits. Big and loud, he was always complaining and making dirty remarks to the staff. Janice had walked into his bedroom once and caught him combing the hair around his privates. It was rumoured that he liked to wear it in a centre parting.

His eyes were no better, I noticed. They were bloodshot with a gungy secretion in the corners. *Conjunctivitis: Inflammation of the conjunctiva*, was what it said in my Medical Dictionary. Janice had offered to clean them last week. She'd taken my advice and made up a saline solution of one part household salt to three parts warm water, but hadn't been able to get near him. When she asked if he had a couple of cotton wool balls, he pushed her away and cried, Whit dae ye think ah am? A bliddy teddy bear?

That's a vulgar, vulgar man, said mammy, who liked repeating adjectives for effect.

I examined Macum. He was busy sloshing more tea into his saucer.

Lily, stop staring. It's bad manners. She smiled politely at me, stretched her eyes, then went to help Janice gather in the empty cups.

Nana, I whispered. Do you think we could go somewhere more private? Just the two of us. Your room maybe? There's something I need to ask before mammy comes back.

Eh – we can't Lily. We're no allowed to smoke there.

I stifled a sigh. How anyone could prefer to sit in this choking atmosphere when there was somewhere else to go was beyond me. But, unlike most of my family, I wasn't addicted to nicotine.

You're no allowed to do anything in this place, she continued, as soon as mammy returned. It's like being in jail. Ah'm telling you Grace. The Tallies were treated better up at the camp during the war.

I'd been to the Tallie camp a few times walking with my friend Maureen and had seen the rows of huts with their windows boarded up. It was used for keeping hens in now. We could hear them squawking when we walked by. One day we crept over the fence, prised a plank loose and keeked inside. There were hundreds of birds crammed together, flapping their wings and jostling for space. Some of them had pecked themselves bald – as if they'd decided to get themselves ready for the pot and save the farmer the bother. It made me want to cry. The stink was so bad we had to hold our breaths then run for air. We'd wanted to sneak back when it grew dark and set them free, but we didn't know where to put them.

This place – it's no the same as your own house, Nana gazed at us wistfully. It's too hot, and that shower contraption in the bathroom would drill a hole in you. Ah've never seen anything like it in all ma natural days. Ah'm no as tough as ah used to be you know. Ma skin's like tissue paper. Ah'd rather have a bath any day. There's clumps of stuff in the drain. The very linoleum's coated with hair. It's a dampt disgrace!

It can't be as bad as all that. Mammy cast her eyes at the ceiling.

Ah'm telling you – it is. May God strike me dead if ah tell a lie.

They lit another couple of cigarettes and Nana told her how she'd been smittled with diarrhoea last week and ended up stuck on the pan for over an hour with no paper. Mammy sat and nodded patiently.

Why didn't you ring the emergency bell?

Ah tried Grace, but it wasn't working.

I'll have a word with someone about it on the way out.

Oh you needn't bother. It's fixed now. Nana made a sucking noise with her cheeks. Ah press it every ten minutes or so, just to make sure.

Mammy stood up. I'm just going to nip to the bathroom.

As soon as she left, I pulled my stool closer.

Nana, there's something I need to tell you. It's about –

Ah'm no keen on their methods in here Lily. Her eyes misted over and her mouth began to tremble. The staff are always making you *do* things.

67

I looked at her in alarm. What kind of things?

Somebody's coming in to give dance classes next week. She swallowed hard. We've all to take part.

That'll be nice. I grinned brightly. People used to come for miles to see you and grandpa dance. Remember all the medals and trophies you won?

I had a sudden vision of Nana gliding across the floor. She was wearing a gold lamé dress with a fish-tail hem and my grandfather was dressed in a silk waistcoat, his black hair sloping across his brow. Their movements were quick and fluid as, cheek to cheek, they danced the tango. Cellos and violins strummed as they whirled around, strutted forward, broke apart and came together again. She retreated, arched backwards and paused for a moment as his eyes burned into hers. Slowly he drew her close, pressed her to his throbbing heart, then whirled her around again.

You'll be able to show them a thing or two, I added. I can't wait to see their faces when you do the tango.

It's no that kind of dancing.

Oh, what kind is it then?

Nana coughed and stared at her slippers. It's called music and movement. All they do is put on a Jimmy Shand record and throw a bean bag at you.

Mammy appeared again and perched on the stool. An empty feeling came over me. I thought about helping myself to another biscuit, sneaked a look at her, and decided against it.

We used to have music and movement at primary school, I remarked, after a while. It was good fun. They play a tune, and if it's big and noisy with lots of drums, you have to stamp about and pretend you're an elephant or something like that. And if they play violins and piccolos you stand on tiptoe and run around like a fairy.

As soon as I stopped talking it went quiet. So still, I could hear the blood rumbling in my ears. Mammy's eyes grew wide and glassy as she studied the daisy pattern on the carpet. I looked at Nana. She was staring out at the rain, her teeth clicking like a pair of castanets. All at once, she wiggled to the edge of the couch and grasped her zimmer. Mammy helped her to her feet. She held on for a second to gain her balance and muttered, Ah'll have to go. It's time for ma tablets.

For some reason, the swallowing of pills at certain intervals throughout the day had become a major event. Old people were strange, I thought. They were proud of their arthritis, bragged about their medication and loved talking about their operations.

I'm going to have a word with Matron. Mammy lifted her message bag and hooked an arm through the handles. Lily, I'd like you to help Nana get ready for bed. I won't be long.

Nana began making her way slowly along the corridor, waving the zimmer around in front of her like a metal detector. I could hardly believe my luck. I'd been waiting so long for an opportunity to talk to her alone that I had to fight the urge to toss the thing aside and drag her into the lift.

Minutes later we arrived in her room.

Look at me, she sniffed, clomping across the carpet and lowering herself onto the edge of the bed. Ah'm bent double. You could vernear use me as a footstool. Here's ma falsers, Lily.

I grabbed a tumbler of water and she plopped them in.

Nana, I've got something to tell you.

Now remember. Just half a Steradent. They last twice as long that way.

I broke the tablet and watched the teeth as they hissed and grinned through the glass.

Nana – listen –

Help me undress Lily. Ah'm awfy tired.

I stripped off her frock and stockings and for a moment imagined I could smell Florence my pet rabbit. I couldn't help noticing how much weight she'd lost. Her arms and legs looked as though they might snap at any moment. What had once been breasts were now empty bags of skin that flopped onto a belly so swollen it looked as though she'd eaten a football. Below it the flesh hung in pleats and settled in a skirt around her hips.

I pulled a pair of waterproof knickers with elasticated legs from the drawer and inserted a pad into the special slit in the crotch.

What in the name of God are those! Nana pointed a bony finger at them.

They're your Kanga pants Nana. Don't you remember? I hauled them up to her waist and tucked her vest inside the way she liked.

She shook her head, grinned at me and began humming a tune. I pulled her upright, took her left hand in mine and she started to chuckle. She placed an arm around my waist and we began to waltz slowly across the floor.

Come on and do the Kanga! Come on and do the Kanga! Na na na na! Na na na na! As we twirled between the wardrobe and the dressing-table, I caught sight of the two figures in the mirror. A frizzy-haired freak in battered old trainers, and an old woman with a big gummy smile that seemed to light up the air around us. Nana's giggle cracked suddenly and changed to a kind of cackle, but I didn't care. She hadn't laughed like that for a long time.

I eased her down gently, lifted her ankles and swivelled her onto the bed.

Nana, I need to speak to you.

What's that?

I waited till her breathing slowed.

You have to leave this place right away. I really miss you. There's no one to talk to at home.

Her eyes slid away from mine and settled on the clock above my head.

Och, ah don't think —

Please! I cupped her face in my hand. Held her eyes in mine. I want you to tell mammy that you're coming to live with us again. She told a lie before — when she said everything was fine. Things have changed since you left. They shout bad words — horrible things to each other. Dad says she's selfish because she doesn't want look after you any more. Especially since you came and took care of her after I was born when she kept crying and going for long walks in her slippers. But it's my fault really. I didn't try to help. Only — I'm at the big school now. In some of the classes they show you how to cook. It's called Food and Nutrition. I can peel potatoes and make the tea. I don't care if you pee your pants and spit on the carpets. I'll clean it up.

Please Nana! Dad's going to the pub nearly every night. He's started being late for work and taking days off. Mammy says that we don't have any money.

But, I don't know – Her lower lip began to wobble.

Listen! I reached for her hand. You're his mother. You could talk to him. Do you remember my friend Maureen? Well, her sister saw him with a woman last Saturday. She told Maureen and Maureen told me. They were coming out of a pub in town. She says that she's blonde and beautiful and looks like Marilyn Monroe, but she doesn't. I sneaked up to her house one night and spied on her. She's not beautiful at all. Those red stilettos she wears went out with the ark. And she's needing her roots done.

Ah'm no sure. Her voice sounded small and thin.

Mammy calls her his f – fancy wife. But she doesn't look very fancy to me. Please Nana! I felt the burn of tears in my eyes. If you come home everything will be the way it was before. Last week she took a dizzy turn and fell down the stairs. She had to have stitches in her head. I saw the wee black dots on her scalp today, underneath her rainmate where the hair had folded up. You could sign yourself out of here, right now. All you have to do is tell Matron and she'll fetch your coat.

I inhaled slowly and waited.

So – what do you think Nana?

Och, ah don't know. Ah just don't know.

There was a long silence. She kept rolling her hands together, palm over palm as if washing with invisible water. I took hold of them, held them fast, felt her fingers scratch like thorns against mine. My throat ached as if I had been running up a hill. Nana appeared to be glued to the bed. I sat with my heart thudding painfully in my chest, and listened to the crows screeching and flapping outside the window.

Finally, she stirred. She raised herself slowly, and edged closer, her silver hair spreading like frosted wings across the pillow. The seconds ticked by as she peered at me, her mouth working in a circle. It seemed to take a long time before the words came out, but at last she spoke.

Your face is awfy familiar, she said. You're no a MacGrorie are ye?

Just the Way He Liked It

Teresa R Funke

Rick smiled at the leggy brunette in the front seat, then turned his attention back to the fuzzy white line in the road. He didn't want to lose his buzz – it had been too good a night to slow down now – but he didn't want to do anything stupid, either. As far as he was concerned, it was something of a miracle this pretty woman in her sexy black miniskirt and pink stretch top had agreed to come home with him. And being a good Catholic boy, he wasn't one to mess with miracles.

He noticed she'd grown quiet as they drove farther from the downtown bars and wondered what she was thinking. If she changed her mind, he'd take her home, of course. He'd never forced himself on anyone. But, God, how he hoped he wouldn't have to do that. It'd been more than a month since he'd had sex, and listening to his roommate and his girlfriend and their drunken sex games had lately gotten him thinking about the raunchy bars down in Garden City. He'd withstood the urge to try them tonight, though. In the back of his mind, the very back, he was starting to think marriage, and the seedy bars were no place to find a wife. That's how he'd wound up at The Storm tonight. That's how he'd wound up with her.

"Great band," he said again.

"Best in town. I go wherever they're playing." She smiled through deep red lipstick, and it was good to see that smile.

"Did you say you grew up in Stanley?" he asked.

"Yeah. Small town. Nothing to do. Got out as fast as I could."

"Don't I know it," he said, maneuvering a blind curve. "From a small farming town myself. Mom cried the day I left for college, but I cranked the music and grinned like an idiot the whole four-hour drive."

They laughed.

Her name was Robyn, and she had a great laugh. Not one of those squirrelly giggles that some women play on a first date, but a genuine, back-of-the-throat laugh. He could stand to hear a bit more of that. Yep, he could stand a bit more of her in many ways.

As he pulled into the driveway of his apartment complex, she laughed again and mentioned that she used to live here. She leaned forward and looked with interest at each of the buildings.

"Which was yours?" he asked.

"B12. I see the Hacker still lives below."

He slowed to get a look. "Who's the Hacker?"

"Chain smoker. Older guy. Every morning he'd step onto his back patio and hack up something horrible. It was the most revolting sound to wake up to. He's one of the reasons I moved out."

"Good reason." He'd just parked the car in front of his building when he remembered she'd been drinking mixed drinks all night, and all he had in the fridge was beer. He was wondering if he could bum some vodka off the college boys downstairs when he heard her say, "Do you live on the first or second level?"

"Second."

"Well, then, who's that girl sitting on your stairs? She's waving at us."

Rick leaned forward to peer around Robyn. It took him a moment to focus his vision, or maybe he just didn't want to see what he was seeing. "God dammit," he said.

"You know her?"

He settled back hard in his seat, hands squeezing the steering wheel till he thought he felt metal give. "Yeah, I know her." He worked to clear his mind 'cause he'd have to think straight to get out of this one without a scene. "I used to date her. She must have left something at the apartment," he said, keeping his voice as steady as his growing rage would allow.

Robyn looked uneasy. She'd told him she was a psychology major in college, and he wondered if that meant she was good at sizing up people. If so, the last thing he needed was for her to meet Valerie.

"Stay right here. Give me a minute to get rid of her and we'll head upstairs. Okay?"

73

"Yeah fine." She pulled her skirt down toward her knees and held it there.

"Okay, then. *Right* here."

He dropped out of the cab of the Chevy S10, and as soon as his heavy cowboy boots hit the pavement, he felt the urge to rush Valerie, to drag her off the stairs and behind the building. Instead, as he rounded the front of the pickup, he tapped the hood to get Robyn's attention. She looked at him, and he held up an index finger, a just-one-second gesture meant to reassure her but also to remind him what his goal was and to let Valerie know exactly where he stood.

At least she was out in the open this time. A few months back when he'd convinced Valerie they should try dating others, he'd brought a girl home and was stunned when Valerie sprang out of the bedroom and launched herself onto the girl's back. He'd met that rancher's daughter at the country bar on the edge of town and, as it turned out, she was more than able to take care of herself. By the time he'd pulled them apart, Valerie was much the worse for the encounter. As his foot hit the bottom stair, he paused, recalling how Valerie's skin had peeked through her torn blouse that night and how they'd found pieces of hair from the rancher's daughter wrapped up in Valerie's ring.

Valerie wet her lips as she leaned against the banister. She was standing halfway up the staircase wearing a tight dress with plenty of cleavage showing below her open Levi jacket. She raised up on her toes, and he noticed she was wearing the high-heeled sandals he'd bought her for Christmas, the ones she'd insisted had better be under the tree. She folded her arms under her breasts and pushed up. Despite himself, he smiled.

"Who's the girl in the car, Ricky?"

He cleared his throat and got serious. "None of your business, Valerie. Get the fuck off my stairs."

"What language, Ricky. But then you farm boys are a crude lot. That's what I like about ya."

She trailed her finger down his button-down shirt, but he slapped it away, glad that his back was to Robyn in the truck. He'd grown to appreciate that being a big man had its advantages. In this case it meant, from her vantage point, Robyn probably couldn't see much of Valerie at all.

"Now's not the time, okay?" he said. "I'll walk you to your car. Maybe we can talk tomorrow."

"Sorry, Ricky. No car."

"Then how'd you get here?"

"I walked, silly."

He raised an eyebrow. "From your place? In those shoes?"

"I needed the exercise." She reached to touch his hair, but he snapped his head back. "I had to see you, lover," she said. "It's been too long."

"Oh, believe me, a month's not long enough," he said, leaning in for emphasis. He could smell the beer on her breath.

She tipped her head back and laughed, and the sound drew his hands into fists. He grabbed her arm, but she wrenched free and raised her other hand. Something flashed, and instinctively he tripped back down a couple of stairs. His gaze focused on the sharp metal object in her hand and then shifted to her face just long enough to catch the curl of her lips. The fact that she was enjoying this drew all reason from his mind. He charged up the stairs toward her. "Come at me, you crazy bitch. Just give me an excuse."

She scrambled backward up the stairs. "Ricky, I would never hurt you." She raised her free hand and pushed it hard against his chest. "You know how much I love you."

His right eye began to twitch, and he pressed his palm against it. "Those are my scissors," he said. "How'd you get them?"

"From your apartment, of course. Oh, and I finished off your beer. I'll buy you a half case later."

He shook his head. "But I took back my key."

He grabbed at her jacket, and again she dodged.

"Careful," she said, breathing hard. "Your friend is watching."

In the couple of seconds it took Rick to glance over his shoulder, two things happened. He noticed Robyn getting out of the truck, her eyes fixed on Valerie, and he heard a strange thud. He turned back to see Valerie holding the handles of the scissors now imbedded in her right

75

thigh. She was sinking down onto the steps, her face white but her eyes flashing. It took him a moment to register what had happened.

He knelt down on the step just below her, his hands hovering around the scissors, unsure what to do as the blood began to streak her bare leg. "Jesus, Valerie."

"Have I got your attention?" she asked, beads of sweat gathering at her temples. "'Cause I need to tell you something, Baby. I don't wanna be alone again. And I'll do whatever it takes to keep you around. Just tell me what you want."

Robyn was at the foot of the stairs. His eyes met Valerie's for a moment, then he stood to block Robyn.

"Oh, my God. She just stabbed herself," Robyn said as Rick took her elbow and guided her back down the stairs. Robyn's eyes were darting toward the other buildings, toward the sound of a car door slamming. Valerie let out a long, low moan, and Robyn shuddered.

"You know it's not the craziest thing she's ever done," Rick said. "That'd be the time she stopped her car on the railroad tracks when a train was coming," he forced a chuckle then realized too late that making light of this was the wrong thing to do. From the way she avoided his gaze and drew her arms around herself, Rick knew he'd finally made that mistake he'd been trying to avoid. With a sigh, he reached into his pocket and pulled out his keys. "Take my truck home," he said. "You can drop it off tomorrow. I'll use my roommate's car to get her to the hospital."

"Are you sure? I can call a cab."

"No, take it."

Robyn didn't hesitate. She snatched the keys from his hand and hurried to the driver's side. She paused, searching for words.

He spared her the trouble. "Drive safe," he said.

She nodded and pulled away from the curb without a backward glance. And she was gone, and all that was left was Valerie and a sick feeling in his gut that was only partly the start of a hangover.

"Hey, lover boy," Valerie said. "Did you forget about me?"

"Shut up, Valerie. Just shut the fuck up." As he brushed past her on the stairs, he jutted a finger in her face. "Wait right there," he said. "I don't want blood in the house."

76

He kicked empty beer cans out of the entryway and went straight to the bathroom to get an Ace bandage, then to the kitchen for dishtowels. As he headed for the door, he remembered to grab his roommate's keys off the counter. When he came back, he noticed Valerie's head rolled back, her eyes closed and her mouth open, and he wondered how he was supposed to revive her if she'd fainted. It might be nice to have an excuse to slap her. But she opened her eyes and smiled weakly as he lowered himself beside her.

His hands shook a little as he reached for the scissors.

"I think you're supposed to leave them in till we get to the ER," she said, her breath coming in sharp pants.

"Then how do I stop the bleeding?"

"I don't know. Can you make a tourniquet?"

"Do I look like a goddamn doctor? Jesus, Valerie, *look* at this!"

And they both stared at the scissors and the blood now washing over her trembling thigh and dripping steadily onto the step below.

"Do you think it hit bone?" he asked, fascinated despite himself.

"Feels like it. Feels like my whole leg is comin' off."

"I can't believe you didn't scream. I know guys with less balls than you." He pushed her hair out of her eyes.

Rick wrapped the dishtowels around the scissors, doing his best to tie them down with the Ace bandage. It didn't look as good as he thought it should, but being so close to her, touching her this way, was beginning to make him queasy. He stood up and wiped his hands on his jeans.

"Can you walk?"

"Stupid question." She was crying freely now.

"Shit," he said, wiping his forehead with the back of his bloody hand. "All right, put your arms up."

She raised her arms to him and drew them tight around his neck as he bent to lift her. He was always surprised how easily she came up. People had often commented on the difference in their sizes, as if that were the reason they were mismatched. But it had never bothered Rick. In fact, he liked how easily he could pack her around, how he could pin her arms behind her when she got too rough. It was the sense of control he needed with Valerie.

When he lifted her, Valerie winced and buried her head in his shoulder. He paused, then stepped carefully down the stairs, wishing he'd had the sense to unlock his roommate's car. Now he had to bend forward as Valerie struggled with the lock. "Oh, Ricky," she said, pulling up on his neck when the door was open. "It hurts like hell."

"Serves you right," he said, dropping her onto the front seat and reaching into the back to grab his roommate's sweatshirt. She moaned as he lifted her leg and slid the sweatshirt underneath.

"Better the shirt than the upholstery," he said. "You know how Tom is."

Valerie nodded vigorously, even managed a slight chuckle. The best thing about Valerie was that she knew his life intimately. He never had to explain anything to her. There was some comfort in that, even in moments like this – maybe especially in moments like this. He closed the door and got into the car.

She was looking very pale now. He put his hand on her left knee. "You okay, Val?"

"What happened to all those... pet names you had for me?" she asked. "You never call me those... anymore."

He turned the key in the ignition. "The only thing I ever called you was Crazy Bitch and, at the moment, that would only seem redundant."

She turned her head away from him and squeezed her eyes as if to shut out the pain. His stomach was churning from hunger and alcohol and disgust with Valerie and with himself. How had he ever let it come to this? Why hadn't he broken off with her months ago? But then, it wouldn't have mattered when he did it. She would always have reacted this way. Maybe that's what took him so long.

They were quiet as he sped toward the hospital, no longer attentive to lines in the road or red lights or traffic. In the stillness, with the sound of her shallow breathing and the smell of blood in the car, he started to see the scene as if from outside himself, and only then did he fully realize just how sick this whole mess really was. He saw it through Robyn's eyes, and he knew it would be like this with the next girl and the next until he could finally drive Valerie out of his life.

At the ER, they put Valerie on a gurney and rushed her into an examining room. Rick started to follow, but a nurse escorted him toward the chairs in the waiting area. He sat there watching the clock tick off three a.m., and then a police officer arrived. Rick expected a breath test but didn't get one. He expected the third degree but didn't get that either. Turned out the officer was only filling out an information report. He'd already talked to Valerie and was only confirming her story. When their stories synced up, he seemed satisfied. He acted like he saw this sort of thing all the time, and Rick wondered if he should feel comforted by that. He rolled his shirtsleeves up as he walked the officer outside.

Rick stayed in the cool night air and considered going home, but something (it could only have been the voice of his mother) told him to stay, to at least make sure she was okay. The doctor found him leaning against the brick wall shooting the breeze with an orderly who'd come out for a smoke.

"Are you Rick?"

"That's right."

"She's asking for you."

Rick looked past the doctor toward the room where Valerie lay. "Is she all right?"

"She will be. The angle of the scissors caused a severe laceration to her skin and thigh muscle. We've stitched her up. She's lucky. If she had hit an artery, it would have been much worse. I've called for a psych council."

"Good idea."

"They could be awhile, though. Might help if you sat with her till they arrive."

Rick rubbed his neck. "I think maybe I oughta go, Doc. It's late, and you said she's okay."

The doctor looked at the ground. "I think she'd be less agitated if you stayed."

"Shit," Rick said. "It's never gonna end."

The doctor said nothing, just put his hands in the pockets of his white coat and waited to see what Rick would do.

"Okay, but only till the shrink arrives."

The doctor nodded and showed him to Valerie's room.

At first Rick thought she was sleeping. Her eyes were closed, and she looked completely relaxed. He was turning to leave when he heard his name. Her hand was outstretched, and he stepped slowly toward it. He hesitated before he took her hand.

"Doctor says you'll be okay. That's good, huh?"

"Doesn't matter. If I don't have you, nothing matters."

With his foot, he pulled up a chair. He didn't want to be cruel, but he wanted to be clear. "Val, I told you last month, it's over. Nothing's gonna change that. Not even this. I'm sorry, okay? But that's the way it's gonna be."

Her gaze went to the ceiling, and Rick got ready for the waterworks, but she turned back to him with anger in her eyes. "Why do *you* get to decide when it's over?"

He dropped her hand. "Because I do."

She pushed herself up on the pillows to look him straight in the eye. "Why now, Rick? Why after two years? If I'm so repulsive, what kept you with me so long?"

"The sex, of course," he sneered.

"Bullshit. A man'll stay with a woman for sex for a few months, but not two years."

He rose to pace, running his hands through his hair and down to the back of his neck. "Okay, maybe I wanted someone to play with my mind. All your head games, the whacked-out things you did kept it interesting for a while, made it a little dangerous. Maybe I liked the attention I got, all the concern from my parents and friends who thought you were nothing but trouble."

"You should've shot up drugs, then. You'd have gotten the same rush and a hell of a lot more attention."

"Valerie, it doesn't *matter* why I stayed. What matters is I want out. I'm twenty-five. I'm doing well at work. And there was that scare with my Dad a few weeks back. It all gives me some perspective, okay? I think maybe it's time I get my shit together."

She applauded. "Very touching. Now let me tell you why you want out," she said. "You're bored with me. I can understand that. I just need to juice things up a bit, bring back the magic. I think tonight proved I've still got a few tricks up my sleeve."

"Tonight was psycho, Valerie."

"Just the way you like it. I saw the look in your eyes when I put the scissors in. I felt your arms tremble when you carried me. Even your girlfriend could see you were worked up. It doesn't get any better than tonight, baby. Now I *know* you love me."

"You're a head case," he said. "The shrink's gonna nail you to the wall."

"Oh, please. You think I can't talk my way around a shrink?"

"Stay away from me, Valerie. I mean it. I'll get the cops involved if I have to."

She laughed, and it was one of those loud, rattling cackles that made his skin crawl. "The cops?" she said. "So you're ready to admit you're not man enough to handle me alone?"

He came back to the bed and leaned in close. "I'm more than man enough, Valerie. Next time I'll let you bleed to death."

She laid a hand on his cheek. "Poor baby," she said, tears welling in her eyes. "I put you through so much."

He reached up and pulled her hand away, gripping her wrist for a moment before he turned to go.

"Ricky," she called. "Don't forget your scissors. They're probably holding them at the desk. You know, I thought they were a little dull. I could come by and sharpen them for you. I'll get those bloodstains out of your clothes, too. Just give me a day or two to get back on my feet."

As she spoke, his legs grew heavy. He wanted to run from that room, but his body was weighing him down. It was past four a.m., and he felt like he hadn't slept in days. As he slumped down the hall, he heard her begin to sing the song she always called "their song." He put his hands to his ears. But as he got farther from her door, he remembered the night they'd danced to that song. She'd been wearing a sleeveless black dress that looked more like a slip, and her hair had been teased up just the way he liked it. She'd let him feel her up on the dance floor and they'd gone out back to have sex in his car. God, she'd been a wild one that night. He pushed the thought from his mind, just as he would push her from his life. Black dress or no black dress, he would. This he promised himself — again.

81

Saba Is Sentenced to Death by Stoning

Virginia McRea

This is what I was told by someone who was there, a journalist who doesn't want his name to be used.

The woman's name was Saba, and she was thirty years old and a citizen of Iran. She had committed adultery – there is no doubt about this, as both she and the man acknowledged it – and for that crime she was sentenced to be lashed and then executed by stoning. This happened not in the middle ages but quite recently.

The man's name was Hossein. Fortunately for him, he was unmarried. Had he been married, legally he could have been stoned, too. Instead, he was sentenced to one hundred lashes. Money changed hands, however, and in the end he was merely sent back to his native village, with the stones to be used to kill Saba heaped up in his heart forever.

Why blame him for what happened? Why blame her? They were minding their own business when fate busily intervened. At the suggestion of his uncle, whom fate elected to sow trouble, Hossein had shown up at Saba's husband's bakery, looking for work. Soon he and Saba lay together in the storehouse on sacks of flour, as if lying on carpets in a garden. In the moonlight stealing through barred windows, mice – gentle handmaidens – sang to them, and danced. The couple's sighs and whispers, the sounds of their breathing, were baked into every round of bread. Everyone said the bread was sweeter than it used to be; maybe that's what tipped off the husband. He burst in and found them, and that was the end of one thing and the beginning of another.

As is usual in such cases, the religious judge ordered the husband to attend the execution and even to throw stones. The husband said, with commendable enthusiasm, that he surely would, but when the day arrived, he failed to show up. Money had changed hands, and a doctor had been found who agreed to certify that he was critically ill and bedridden. No one was fooled. He was ashamed to be seen in public, because of his wife's deception; he felt that it reflected on his manhood, which actually, in this case, it did.

Again, as is usual in such cases, the religious judge also ordered the children to attend – a small boy and a girl of nine or ten. The idea was for them to profit by witnessing their mother's "repentance." Well, why not? The Islamic Penal Code in force in Iran allows girls as young as nine to be stoned, or so one is told, so why should they not witness a stoning? The father was in favor of it, but the maternal grandmother was not. Money changed hands, and the children were abducted and sequestered for the time being in the grandmother's home.

The crime. The sentence. The execution. These are words with an aura of procedure, legality, and justice, and indeed, the whole thing is perfectly legal. One speaks here not of kangaroo courts and lynch mobs, but of due process. One speaks of the law, and respect for the law, and of the law's being followed to the letter.

At many times, in many places, adultery has been a crime. In modern Iran, it is known as a "moral offense." Like prostitution, it is punishable by stoning. The Penal Code (or the Law of Hodoud) calls for punishment by one hundred lashes for unmarried men and women, and stoning for those who are married.

One would like to think that stonings do not happen very often, if at all. Unfortunately, in Iran, in the past twenty years, they have happened hundreds of times, or so it is said. Of course, one is free to ignore what is said. People have their political agendas, they have axes to grind. Still, stonings are known to have happened; the authorities acknowledge this. They are known to have happened more than once.

The regime alleges that stonings, on the exceedingly rare occasions when they occur at all, occur only in isolated villages. Not so. Like many reported stonings, Saba's execution is scheduled to be carried out in a city. The place of execution is a public space – not exactly a park, but call it a park – of bare trampled earth where on the day of the execution almond trees are blooming. Above the mad froth of blossoms, the graceful minaret of a mosque pierces the turquoise sky. There is a bus station nearby, and the odor of exhaust mixes with the perfume of the blossoms. There is a racket of buses pulling in and out.

By afternoon men are everywhere, jostling each other in the park and spilling over into the street and obliging the police to redirect traffic. There is not even any room in the park for the pariah dogs. They come as close as they can, yellow snouts to the ground, sniffing, but people throw things at them, pebbles, bottles, whatever they can lay their hands on, and the dogs retreat to a safe distance, lie down with their heads on their paws, and wait.

A truck bumps over the curb of the park; the men whistle, cheer, applaud, give way for the stones. The truck plows through the almond trees, stripping the branches of their blossoms. Toward the front of the park, the truck stops. A huge billboard is hanging there that depicts a rifle-toting mullah; evidently, it is intended as a backstop. Several feet in front of it is a hole in the ground, intended as a sort of grave. To the side, at a dais, several mullahs are sitting, robed, turbaned, ferociously bearded. The driver sticks his head out the window and consults briefly with the mullahs, who nod. He tilts the truckbed and the stones roll out on the ground with a rumble like thunder, raising a cloud of dust. Technically speaking, they are sedimentary stones, cobble conglomerate, commandeered from a road-building project; some are imprinted with fernlike fossils. In accord with the Penal Code, they are "not so large that a person dies after being hit with two of them, nor so small as to be defined as pebbles, but must cause severe injury."

These are perfect – stones of a size a man's hand can cradle, stones around which his fingers can curl.

The truck drives off, and the mullahs signal the men to arm themselves with the stones, which they do greedily, shoving each other out of the way to get at them.

At the sight of the stones, the pariah dogs get up and slink a little closer. They know stones make corpses that can be eaten.

In the distance, horns are honking. Soon a battered limousine heaves into view with Republican guards clinging to the fenders. Outriders in two rusty Jeeps are waving their rifles. This is Saba. What with the noisy welcome, and all the blossoms, and the fancy car, one might think she was a bride being delivered to her wedding. The cavalcade pulls up near the mullahs' table. The guards leap from the Jeeps, and one of them yanks open the limousine's rear door and grabs at Saba. As he drags her out, she bangs her head on the doorframe and catches her foot in the hem of her long black chador. Another guard rushes up, and the two of them grip Saba by the elbows and pull her arms away from her body as if stretching out the wings of a bird. A short, heavyset woman, she stands with her head bowed, suffocating in her veil and chador just as if she were a decent woman.

Men surge up to the car, shake their fists, jeer, shout taunts and curses, flourish the stones. The guards surround Saba and try to push the men back, but they have a hard time of it, flailing at the men with their fists and rifle butts and getting shoved and accidentally hit in the face. Order is restored only when the chief religious judge, who has been sitting at the dais, leaps to his feet and waves his arms and yells commands.

Now the judge has little to do but act as master of ceremonies. The trial, the verdict, the pronouncement of the sentence are all behind him. The rest is up to the executioners.

Three of the guards push Saba to her knees in front of the mullahs' dais and strip her of the veil and chador. Underneath she is wearing a white cotton shift. It is impossible to say whether she is pretty, because no one could be pretty with such an expression of terror on her face. It may be seen, however, that her eyebrows are remarkable – almost unnaturally thick and black, and her eyes are huge. At the sight of her practically naked, the men are transfigured with righteousness, even the mullahs. Their faces shine, their eyes roll back, their eyeteeth gleam. This is really very holy business. And the stones, how impatient they are in their masters' hands, like dogs straining at their leashes! Yes, like roundheaded dogs, thirsty for blood.

Her hands are tied behind her back and she is pushed to her knees. A man wearing civilian clothes struts up to her, brandishing a whip, and begins to lash her back and shoulders. Possibly the thinking is that stoning is too good for her; punitive damages are required. Well, nothing is so bad it could not be worse. In one stoning – in Saudi Arabia – a woman was clubbed instead of lashed, and her shoulders were pulverized. After one hundred lashes, Saba's skin is pulp and the shoulderblades show through, chaste and white.

Now she is half dragged, half carried to the hole in the ground. Before she can be put in, however, she must be enshrouded. While two guards hold her up – she is far too weak to stand – another, starting at her feet, wraps her in a white shroud, stopping under her arms. The meaning of this enshrouding is murky. Maybe the shroud represents graveclothes, maybe it symbolizes repentance or purity, maybe it is intended to hobble her, maybe, after thousands of years of stonings, people have forgotten what it means. In any case, once it is done, the guards lift her under the arms and put her in the hole. According to the law, she is supposed to be buried to her waist, but the hole has inadvertently been dug a bit too shallow, so that she is actually buried to her hips.

Now she is left by herself to face the mob. In her heart, for an instant, surely the word *alone* is raised to its highest power.

Of course, all is not lost. By law, and by ancient custom (well known in biblical times), if she can escape now or at any time during the stoning, she must not be recaptured and may go free. It is unclear how someone with her legs wrapped in a shroud, half buried in a hole in the ground, and hemmed in by a howling mob might manage to escape; nevertheless, it has been done. In one reported case, a woman who had been thrown in a ditch to be stoned, and whose eyes had been gouged out, somehow managed to climb out of the ditch and run off a certain distance. She was, however, recaptured and stoned to death. The mullah who ordered this, on being asked why she had not been allowed to go free, replied that the law absolutely demanded stoning "if her guilt was proven on the basis of witnesses' testimonies," which presumably it was.

It is perhaps necessary to interpolate here that the Penal Code allows not only stoning but also gouging of eyes, crucifixion, mutilation, and amputation.

In any event, Saba does not try to escape.

There is no first stone. Instead, the stones come in a volley that splits her scalp, shatters her front teeth, breaks her jaw and some of her ribs. She shrieks; her hands fly to her face. The stones are heard thumping. Blood pours down her face; she is modestly veiled in her blood. Soon she collapses over the edge of the hole and tries to make herself small. The stoning continues, uninterrupted, for thirty or forty minutes, at which point the religious judge orders it halted temporarily, so that her medical condition may be assessed. Several guards go up to her and with their hands rake away the bloody stones, some stuck with shreds of almond blossoms and sprinkled with shards of teeth. When she has been excavated, a young doctor bustles over, wearing a white coat. Officiously, he stoops down and takes her wrist. Her pulse is still so strong, he says, it throbs like kettledrums. He says the earth beneath him trembles with her pulse.

The religious judge cannot be too careful. He wishes to avoid a repetition of the stoning in which a twenty-year-old woman was eventually pronounced dead, only to revive in the morgue and be sent to the hospital. This incident was reported internationally.

The stoning resumes. Saba shudders and retches and spits out more of her teeth.

How long is long to be killed? Four thousand seconds pass, more than an hour, time enough for light to travel seven hundred million miles. So long that nearly every man in the park has a go at her.

The mullahs confer in a little buzz, decide to stop the stoning again. As before, the guards rake away the stones, revealing something like a little animal run over in the road. The doctor stoops down, takes her broken wrist. He says her pulse is weak, like dripping water. The religious judge says the time has come to cast the last just stones.

Five or six minutes more, and it's over. The doctor applies the stethoscope. Nothing, he says. A lot of cheering breaks out, but secretly the men are infuriated that she's dead already; they would have liked to kill her longer. An epidemic of pushing and shoving ensues as they compete to get near the corpse, kick it, spit on it. One man even reaches for a hand, as if to pull it off. The mullahs know when enough is enough; the proprieties must be observed. They order the guards to shoo the men away. When the guards have done so, they cover the corpse with the chador, as if laying out a cloth on the ground for a picnic. The dogs get up and creep a little closer, frothing like the blossoms.

In sullen packs, the men roam around the park for a while, smoking cigarettes and picking up stones as souvenirs, until, in little groups, they drift away. When they reach their own homes, they shake the bloody stones in their women's faces. Above the veil, eyes widen until the whites show, to the vast amusement of the men, and the women look like nothing so much as skittish goats. *Protect us from our men,* they pray. *Protect us from their stones.* But before the prayers can fly into the ears of God, they are eaten by the veil.

A Fellowship Below Ice
(The Hidden Lives of Lakes)

Gina Ochsner

On a day when the hoarfrost brought the sight line down to a quiver, Glasha and Luba, co-workers at the petrochemical plant and best friends, skidded onto the frozen ice of the lake. They were sitting in a canoe and pushing themselves over the ice, Glasha with her kitchen mop, and sitting opposite of her, Luba with her black rubber toilet-bowl plungers. With each push, Luba knew that Glasha was imagining the pitch of the May Day cheers when she and Luba would glide past the finish line, well ahead of the other canoers. But Luba, who was participating in this folly only because the doctor had told her that her figure was far too Russian, that is to say, fat, was wondering about the thickness of the ice and what might be lying below it. For when she craned her neck over the side of their narrow canoe, Luba could see bubbles trapped in the ice — a disturbing sight because it occurred to her that the bubbles must have come from the fish, which she'd always assumed froze without a struggle, without pain.

When they had reached about a third of the way across the lake Glasha laid her mops over the gunwale and withdrew a silver flask from a coat pocket and uncapped it. From somewhere near the middle of the lake Luba heard a strange humming and for a moment she thought it was the sound of ice threatening to crack. Luba climbed out of the canoe, got on her hands and knees, and pressed her ear to the ice, a thing she'd seen people do in the movies. Then she held the bells of the plungers to her ears. When she did, the humming amplified and separated into the buzz of voices of both men and women. They were speaking in the polite form of Russian, addressing each other in *vuis* instead of *tuis*, speaking with a grace she hadn't heard in town for years. It was a beautiful noise and Luba flapped the plungers at her ears so as to achieve a stereo effect, though she imagined she looked a little like a fish breathing through rubber gills.

"What are you doing?" Glasha capped her flask.

"Here." Luba sat back on her heels and handed Glasha a plunger. "Listen. Do you hear that?"

"What?"

"That whispering." Luba pointed to the ice.

Glasha leaned over the side of the boat and narrowed her eyes.

"It's coming from over there." Luba pointed to the middle of the lake.

"I don't like this," Glasha said quietly. "Let's go."

Luba climbed back into the canoe. Glasha gave a tremendous shove with her mops and sent the boat lurching and all the way to shore, Luba had to work hard to keep up with the steady haul Glasha made with her mops.

That night as her husband Oleg sat finishing a bottle of Crowbar, Luba told him about the voices she'd heard below the ice.

"So what," he said, placing the dead bottle horizontally on the table. Though he was not a big believer in mystery, Luba knew that Oleg was waiting for a minor miracle, some abstruse physical law regarding hidden drops of vodka in a freshly emptied bottle.

"So don't you want to know what they are saying?"

"Not really," Oleg said, turning the bottle upside down and shaking it over a cup.

But in the morning, owing to the fact that it was a Sunday, Oleg had changed his mind.

"Let's take a picnic," he said, ringing up Glasha's husband, Ivan. He and Ivan worked together at the factory assembling the guidance mechanisms to anti-aircraft missiles, though Luba had gathered Oleg felt it was impolite to say so. For years he'd been telling the downstairs neighbors that he and Ivan inserted tiny sprockets in timepieces. Either way, Luba could hardly imagine Ivan capable of such delicate work. He was a large man with a thick torso and wide shoulders. And because he had a red chafing mark below his lower lip, like the raw burns kids get from biting their lip, Luba could not help thinking that despite Ivan's great bulk, there was something permanently childlike about him.

They set out at lunchtime, Glasha with extra blankets, Ivan his two perch poles, and Oleg his fishing net. Behind her, Luba pulled a sled carrying a plunger and their picnic. The gray ice refracted the raw afternoon glare, while the air registered as a cold that crimped through each of Luba's vertebrae. And because ice cannot be trusted, she had to walk bent over like a question mark, her stance broad, her weight carefully distributed over her feet, her eyes looking for the dark ice, which, undermined by mysterious currents, was warmer than the paler stretches. When she saw bubbles in the ice Luba dropped to her knees. She flapped her plunger at her ear and held her breath. Then she heard it again: that quiet murmuring. Luba gave a little shout and signaled the others.

Oleg didn't own a crowbar and had recommended that Ivan bring his. But Ivan had misunderstood and brought vodka instead. It came in handy all the same: with three hundred grams of the stuff and a match they melted a kopeck-sized hole. But still it was only Luba who could hear the voices. For two hours they shaved at the ice with Luba's good butter knife and melted the edges of the hole with their cigarette lighters. Around three o'clock, when the bright disk of the sun tipped on edge and drew the remaining light to a point behind the stand of birch, they'd chipped out a hole large enough for a man to jump into.

What Luba noticed straight off was that the water wasn't grainy and dark the way ice water should be. Rather, it was as clear as the tap water she'd seen running out of the faucets in the kitchens of women in Western commercials. And owing to the width of the hole, Luba could see everything sealed within the strata of ice: near the crust was a tundra swan, its wings outstretched as if the ice had caught it in mid-flight. A few layers below the bird was a used syringe and a lady's evening dress. About half a meter further down, an aria had been trapped in the ice. The notes looked like the dark round seeds within willow pods. When Glasha reached into the hole and picked at the notes with her fingernails, they whittered into flight as a beautiful cry. Farther below, where the ice turned darker in color, was a school of carp, their eyes gazing past her into the distant promise of a summer thaw.

They stood around the hole, studying the water for a few minutes.

"Look!" Glasha waved her gloves frantically. Beneath the transparent lip of ice a pair of shoes, a comb, a child's doll, a broom horse, and a much revered icon of St. Fursa stepping on the devil's leathery wings, gently drifted past. And then, to their surprise, even larger items floated by: a rusted park bench, a statue of Lenin, his bronze coat flying out behind him as if from the force of a winter gale, and a piece of the golden dome of their church, which long ago had been dynamited and sunk in the contaminated bog outside of town.

"How can it be!" Luba cried, for it seemed to her that they were viewing a disassembled version of their town as it was many years ago, an entire town of clutter moving with that slow grace given to things carried by water. There went Old Fedya's ratty prayer ropes; Glasha's missing pig, tins of potted meats, a bottle of watered-down rocket fuel, a chicken, the broken neck of a violin and fibrillating scraps of newspaper moved past them. A T-shirt with a popular saying: *Same Shit, Different Day* whirled up to the surface, along with a pair of Adidas sport pants, the fashionable kind with the white stripe down the side that Luba's daughter had once begged her for.

Oleg dipped his fishing net into the hole and caught the pants as they went swirling by. He shook his head and wrung the excess water from the pants. "All this time we've been canoeing over the lake in summer, we could have been fishing. We'd have been rich by now!"

Ivan licked his thumb, held it to the cold, measuring the lowering frost. Then he dropped his line in. "True enough. But where are all the people?" Ivan balanced an enormous foot on the lip of the hole.

Luba bent over the hole with a plunger at her ear. "Maybe they're afraid of us."

"Maybe we're afraid of them!" Glasha uncapped her flask and took a liberal drink.

"Look!" Ivan hopped from foot to foot. All the grandmothers and grandfathers, children and family pets they'd lost, church members and old friends long departed from the factory, the man from the state office who'd come to examine the caulking around their toilets, drifted slowly past the hole. They were naked, most of them, naked and they never looked better. For they swam about freely under the ice, their movements fluid and smooth. Every now and again, someone would rise so close to the surface, face upturned and eyes frosted over, that Luba thought she might touch them as they floated under the open hole.

Oleg and Ivan dropped in their lines. Immediately Ivan felt a tug and Oleg held him around his waist while he reeled in his catch. It was Manyasha, who'd once lived next door to Glasha and Ivan. They took one look at Manyasha, an indestructible babushka who'd never permitted herself more than a pinched smile, and Ivan tossed her back in.

They fished a while longer and this time Oleg's line went taut. Luba gripped her husband by his belt and leaned back. It took several minutes of hauling up hard, and just when Luba thought she couldn't hold on any more she heard a tremendous splash at the hole. Oleg jumped and dropped his pole. It was Borya, Oleg's uncle, spitting water from his mouth and flailing his arms. At last, he calmed down a bit and managed to remove the hook from his armpit.

"Oh, Uncle Borya!" Oleg knelt and offered Uncle Borya his hand. "I hope we didn't hurt you."

Uncle Borya regarded them for a moment. His eyes were frosted over and Luba couldn't see the pupils of his eyes.

"I always did think you were an idiot, Oleg. But I like your wife. How are things, Luba?" Uncle Borya smiled then and Luba saw that since he'd died he'd lost three more teeth.

"Very good, Uncle." Luba unwound her cobalt blue scarf from around her neck and handed it to Borya. "We are so sorry for disturbing you like this, but, to be honest, we thought you were dead."

Uncle Borya tied the scarf around his neck.

"Everyone thinks that." Uncle Borya narrowed his pasty eyes and studied his nephew. "So now that I'm here, what do you want?"

"Well, I guess we're wondering what you are doing down there." Oleg sat on the ice and handed Borya a flask of Special Export.

"This and that. Mostly I read the dictionary and tell jokes."

"Jokes?" Luba slapped her ear with her mitten, forcing the blood.

"Yes, the Joke Convention meets this time of year. But when we run out of jokes, we become like the carp, very still, and we listen to the ice and life above the ice." Uncle Borya scratched his chin where bits of ice clung to his beard. "Incidentally, would you mind very much bringing me a cabbage pie?" Uncle Borya turned to Luba and winked. "The carp don't taste good this time of year."

"Who else is down there?" Glasha shouldered Luba away from the hole.

"Oh, all sorts of people. You'd be surprised, but then, I'm not supposed to say."

"Why not?" Glasha narrowed her eyes.

Uncle Borya studied the tree line, then bobbed his head up and down. "Excuse me, please, but the Finnish Shouting Choir is about to perform. If you listen you can hear them warming up." Borya pointed to the far end of the lake, then put his hands over his ears and slipped below the water. As if on cue, the Finnish Shouting Choir drifted by en masse, nude save for their choral music, which they clutched to their chests.

They stood for a moment longer peering at the hole in the ice. "Well, that's that." Oleg straightened and brushed ice crystals from the backside of his pants. The last light behind the trees had collapsed to a gritty smear of pollution.

"Yes." Ivan ran his tongue over the raw patch under his lower lip. "Let's go back. There's a good foreign feature playing at the kino." The air had turned to grain, to the kind of night where driving would be forbidden and if they were to get to the movies, they'd have to hurry. As the others trudged ahead, Luba turned back for one last look at the hole. Just then a silver lorgnette, like the one her grandmother had, floated by, a single white lady's glove following in its wake. Luba crouched over the hole. For a moment she imagined drinking the water, or just splashing it over her face to feel the wetness, to feel what it was that kept Uncle Borya so happy for a dead man. Luba dipped the tip of her glove into the water, breaking to fractions the image of her face blinking back at her.

*

Each evening Glasha and Luba chiseled at the hole, both to keep it from freezing back over and also to see what else they might find. The

94

following Saturday, Glasha, Ivan, Oleg and Luba went back out onto the ice. Though Glasha and Ivan liked to drop in a fishing line, Oleg stood ready with the net, hauling up a soggy handkerchief and bottles of herbal vitamins, a real find, which he tossed onto the sled with a quick motion of his wrist. For her part, Luba couldn't bring herself to use a hook and instead swirled the handle of her plunger in the hole. When she felt the handle bump into something, Luba dropped to her knees. There in the water staring back up at her, as a face in a mirror, was Batushka, their beloved priest, dead now for three years. Batushka poked his head through the water.

"That really hurt, you know, but I forgive you."

"Batushka!" Luba cried, tears crusting the corners of her eyes.

"Batushka, if we may," Ivan ventured cautiously toward the hole. "What are you doing down there in the ice? You are dead and buried, at Diveyevo, no?" Ivan asked, for he and Oleg, along with a few others, had carried Batushka's body to his final resting place.

"I can't say," Batushka said with a sad smile.

Glasha lowered her brows. "Not so fast. There's a rule for this. If you catch something, on a hook, say, you have a right to ask it questions and it must answer truthfully."

"You are right." Batushka sighed loudly, reaching for Oleg's bottle of Special Export. "But don't blame me if you don't like the answers I give."

"So what was wrong with Diveyevo?" Ivan asked.

"Oh, that again," Batushka rolled his eyes. "Nothing was wrong with it. I just wish to be humble," Batushka broke flakes of ice and crunched them loudly between his teeth, "to be close to the earth as possible." Under Batushka's fingernails were little clumps of mud from the bottom of the lake, in his ears, bits of grass.

"I don't understand," Oleg pumped his shoulders up and down. "I'm listening, and I'm trying to believe what I'm hearing, but it's not making sense. You're dead. And so are you," Oleg nodded to Borya who'd surfaced just long enough to grab Luba's cabbage pie. "And I'm not dreaming. I'm alive!" Oleg thumped his gloved fist against his chest.

Batushka wagged his head slowly from side to side and made clicking noises with his tongue. "This reminds me of the parable of Josef's chicken. Would you like to hear it?"

"No!" Glasha stamped her feet.

"Then excuse me," Batushka recapped the bottle and slid it across the ice to Oleg, "but I am cold." With that Batushka slipped under the ice.

"But we didn't get to ask all our questions." Ivan's lower lip trembled and Oleg handed him a plastic bottle of vitamins.

"We'll just have to come back, for as long as it takes." Oleg sighed and hitched himself to the sled piled with frozen trinkets. They turned for shore then, Glasha trudging ahead of the men while Luba trailed behind, noting how the strand of lights from the lake's edge were duplicated as dull spots on the ice.

That night Luba lay in bed while Oleg draped his haul over their ancient heating pipes. As she listened to her husband catalogue his inventory, she wondered about the thickness of sleep and ice and the dreams, those trellis-white bones, the townspeople below them might be dreaming. Luba tried to imagine being so humble, so close to the earth, that she'd wake each morning coughing up clay, wiping it from her ears and nostrils. That was grace, the real article, to be washed over, to drown in it.

The following Monday, after work, the four set off again for the center of the lake. Glasha brought several sheets of paper, one for each day of the week, and below the heading, a list of questions ranging from how much longer she'd have to care for her ailing mother to which shops would be carrying butter. Ivan brought a troubling crossword puzzle. Oleg brought a longer fishing net and Luba brought more cabbage pies. When they got there, Glasha called Batushka for nearly an hour while Oleg fished. Crusts of ice lined their eyelashes, the corners of their eyes, and still, no Batushka. At last Oleg hooked his Uncle Borya again, who came kicking and fighting the whole way to the surface of the water.

"Batushka!" Glasha cried. "We came to see Batushka!"

Scraps of newspaper churned to the surface where the wind snatched them up, letters of the heavy line-print falling like seeds onto the ice. "Oh, not to worry," Borya said, watching little black letters from the headlines of the last election rearrange themselves into new words. "He's having a little rest just below the former First Secretaries and the retired gymnasts."

"Well, swim back down there and wake him. It's important." Glasha unfolded her Monday list and tapped her foot impatiently.

In a few moments Batushka chuffed through the hole. His eyes looked especially opaque, and when Luba bent to kiss him on both cheeks, she squeezed her eyes shut, afraid she'd catch a glimpse of her own image returned in the pale orbs of his eyes. Glasha waved her list at Batushka then and they spent a solid hour, taking their turns with Batushka, as they had when he took confession. They left only after Glasha extracted a promise delivered through splayed fingers and yawn – but a promise, no less – that whenever they called for him, Batushka would swim to the surface.

They continued going out to the hole each night for several weeks, Glasha with her lists, Oleg his net, Ivan his crosswords. But it seemed to Luba, the more they asked of Batushka, the vaguer his answers became. Sometimes, he didn't answer at all and broke out instead into silly nursery rhymes. Moreover, with each visit, they came back home smelling more and more like the lake, and Luba couldn't get the smell of carp off her fingers or from out of their flat.

One Friday night, when the moon was a crumpled tissue in the sky, the four set out for the lake.

"Batushka!" Glasha cried as soon as they reached the hole. Then she dropped to her knees. "I want to live life, the way they do in movies!" Glasha threw her hands up, a gesture Luba had seen her practice in front of the mirror in the women's toilets at the petrochemical plant.

"So live, why don't you?" Batushka snapped as he surfaced. "Ask me your question, already."

"This life – what's it for?" Glasha asked, blinking her eyes rapidly.

Batushka's face hardened. He turned his shoulders in the water away from Glasha and looked at the far end of the lake where the birches had grown slender and sparse. "Did you know that people ask much more interesting questions when they are dead?"

Glasha groaned. "Batushka! I'm not happy. What I should do?"

"And did you know," Batushka swung his head around and met her gaze, "that at night the town dreams of itself?" Batushka smiled, a beatific, serene smile.

"This isn't fair! You're not answering my questions." Glasha stomped up and down. Near the hole a small crack zig-zagged from the edge of the ice.

Batushka's eyes brightened. "Each city is a lonely one, knowing it is not right, not complete, longing for something it cannot name." Batushka, still smiling, began to sink slowly into the hole as if someone were gently pulling him down by the heels.

Glasha bent over the hole, cupped her hands around her mouth. "At the very least I want my pig back!" Glasha's words whistled as they dropped to her feet in a small pile of ice crystals.

For several minutes they peered into the hole. Then Glasha turned and stomped toward the shore. Ivan watched his wife for a moment, then hitched himself to Oleg who hitched himself to the sled.

"I'll be glad for the thaw," Oleg said with a pull.

"I always wanted to believe in God, but it never seemed to work out." Ivan leaned into the harness. "Now all I've got are these herbal vitamins," he said, running his tongue over the chafed arc of red skin.

"Vitamins! Well, that's something." Oleg hooked his arm under Ivan's and together they pulled the sled.

That evening Luba lay in bed listening to a dog baying. Outside her bedroom window she could see the frost shortening the horizon, bringing down the moon. She supposed that was what the dog was crying about, singing with a sadness that sounded a little like joy. Luba lay there carried by the sounds of the dog and waited for grace to wash over her, afraid that it never would, had left her completely. But you can't wait forever, that's not living. Luba climbed out of bed and scratched a fingernail into the hoarfrost at the windowpane. Outside the land was pale blue and long with the promise of silent winter and the sure drop of snow.

She thought of those voices, comforting, murmuring conjugations of lost verbs, contemplating the weather and of course, telling their many jokes. Luba smiled. She could just hear it now, the one about the penguins in the movie house and Uncle Borya slapping his thighs in glee. Luba pulled on her thermal underwear, her work uniform, her boots and coat. She tiptoed through the flat and let herself outside where she turned for the lake. She could see her breath freeze before her eyes and fall to the ground at her feet, a gentle sound, the rattling of tiny stars. With each punch of her boots through the crusts of snow, she wondered what it would take to will oneself back to the mud. A baptism among the duck weed and swaying fescue, only this time she wouldn't plug her nose and hold her breath as she had when Batushka held his hand under her back and dipped her down all those years ago. No. She'd plunge in, feet first, her clothes dragging her down into the depths.

Luba walked until she reached the hole. Already it had begun to freeze over, a thin lattice of ice crusting its edges. Luba took off her glove and immersed her hand up to her wrist. It wasn't as cold as she thought it would be for in all their visits to the ice, none of them had ever once gotten wet. Then she heard the voices. They rose steadily, a chorus one after the other, reedy voices canting a wet catechism and the sound was that of old memories.

Luba removed her other glove, her scarf, her hat, her coat, her boots. She would leave behind this clumsy life. The water would remake her, strip her of all that didn't matter. She would trade this dim existence for the embrace of water's quiet where she could contemplate life from below this tormented land. Trade it for the absurdity of floating green skies and a sun filtered through ice.

Pursuit of the Invisible Woman

Sean Lusk

Alex said 'Màiri, you look like a tease,' and that was fine with me. I like being a tease. When I'm feeling fast and dangerous I can really surprise the men; I can make their jaws drop. If I tell them that the damp stain on their tie is Caffrey's, or that the too familiar pubic hair on their fly isn't their own; if I pick it off finely, barely brushing the hissing, static fabric with my shiny red nails, that is when I make their jaws drop. Then I say 'Marmite for breakfast!' and their mouth snaps shut like a fish's mouth, all tiny sharp jagged teeth.

Understand this: I know that this vision of mouths is one of my wrong visions.

I know that teeth are smooth and square like white tombstones. I've run my tongue around the inside of enough mouths to know the feel and size of them. Hot mouths and cool mouths. Tongues big and loose, like slabs of warm meat; tight little firm tongues, reptilian and bloodless. Mouths tasting of tobacco or lunchtime beer. Mouths tasting of other mouths, mouths tasting of death, or as if something just died inside them. But the mouths I see are small and red and sharp, they are gasping and needy.

These are some of my other wrong visions:

Wednesdays bathed in green light; pigeons possessed of tiny human heads; books gently swaying and moaning and coaxing as they sit on shelves; stars bearing their names as they fly through the night sky, *Polaris, Orion*, as if these were their real names, pinned, badged, fixed, (as if any of our names were anything more than unwanted gifts we are obliged to unwrap in front of the whole world). Cucumbers crying human tears, farts billowing in pink clouds behind their donors. I know all these visions to be wrong but they are true to me, and I am not sorry.

People think the streets must be more dangerous for me than for the other girls, but how can this be true? I stand in the darkest corner and see who's coming before they even know what they're looking for. The muscles tense in their calves and their heels draw up inside their shoes as they draw near, so near that I can taste their hopes. They are such pitifully small things, other people's hopes, vesicles which rattle about inside of them, waiting to burst. They hope *to be touched gently, to not be found out, to have hair, to be told they are fine, to sleep, to have a friend, to feel no pain, to forget.*

If I walk towards them they stop giving me these clues about themselves; they become like a step, or a road sign, or a flashing light. I try to stand still; I keep my composure.

I am keeping my composure now, sitting in the deep silence of the church, breathing in its cool smell, running the palm of my hand over the surface of my life, feeling every kink in its weave catching me, reminding me. I hear the sound of a door shutting, not any painted door, but the heavy wooden door at the far end of the nave of the church and I know what the door will do even before it is pushed. I understand its hinges and wait for the gust of air the door makes as it swings, longing for the rush of it past the back of my neck. As the door meets the frame there is a moment's pause before the echo of collision hurtles up the nave, filling the ears of every golden angel and stone devil, hurling itself down the top of the organ pipe and up the cassock of the priest. It's an ending.

I hear her again, with her old woman shuffle shuffling by. I do not know who she is, will not ask her name. She thinks I don't know that she's circling me; don't know she thinks she's the vulture. I hear her heels dragging along lower than her toes so that her outdoor slippers are worn away at their backs. I can even hear the holes that sag at the knees of her thick tights. She's always coming in here. I'd like to tell her to fuck off, but I keep my composure. I pray for him and I am never disturbed.

Everyone says I have a very visual imagination. The girls say 'Màiri, you have a very visual imagination' and in my mind's eye I see them smile as they say it, for it makes them happy, this idea of me seeing so much,

101

but never quite so much as them.

I did not know that I was unable to see my world in the way you see yours until I was five years old. This might seem surprising to you, but how was I to know if no one told me?

Dad said 'Màiri, see that bird,' and described its blue and grey feathers, its moleskin head, its tiny yellow eyes, its hard stubby beak, and I saw the bird. Mum showed me the family album: pictures of granny and grandad, of great grandparents, of relatives I'd never see, the living and the dead. She described their clothes and their faces, the tight moustaches and slicked back hair of the men and the cupid bow lips and polka dot dresses of the women, and I saw them too.

I liked to look at pictures with Alex, to have him show them to me. I would allow myself to relax a little inside his patience; his breath on my ears and cheek, the blood in his thigh beating against the blood in mine, separated by imploring skin and dumb hairs. Understand: once I've seen pictures they are mine, more mine than any picture of yours. I am the blind woman with the photographic memory. Perhaps there are others like me, but I have not yet met my mirror image, so I believe I am the only one.

At home, when I was small and before I understood that I was blind, I would go back to the family album when I thought no one was looking and I'd run my fingers over the photographs. The oldest ones were grainy and dry; the newer had a feeling of being always slightly wet. I'd stare at them for hours until I knew exactly what everyone looked like: the old ladies with their smell of geraniums and the men with haloes of oily rags; young aunts in mini skirts looking like typewriter oil. The colour photos thin and unreal, wobbling between now and then. I sensed them watching me sometimes. I'd feel their eyes staring into mine and think of our shared sightlessness.

Mum and Dad watched me. A waste of watching I'd think to myself, feeling their gaze on the back of my neck. But I never said, just in case they stopped. I am not an attention seeker, but this does not stop me growing warm in the centre of attention.

They tried to make up for my sightless eyes, these stumbling parents of mine, first by telling me what my world looked like, then by getting me to tell them what theirs looked like, our world, and in this way they got me to believe I could see. I have never worked out why they waited so long to tell me I could not. Perhaps it was because they did not want to disappoint me; perhaps it was their own disappointment they were trying to avoid. And so they spent my first few years chasing each other, never quite reaching the point where they had to admit this truth, among all their other undisclosed truths. Perhaps they thought that I would suddenly gain the power of sight; God knows they believed in miracles. They left it so long that I did not understand how to see and how not to see; I still don't understand, despite the frequency with which I walk into furniture, low walls and small, erratic dogs.

It created trouble, this ignorance of mine, this seeing everything so differently to everyone else. Dad would get me to drive when we went out in our Zephyr. How I loved that name; Dad said it was a very old car, worth nothing at all, but to me it was heaven, with its smells of warm well-used vinyl, of dashboards and of a cigar lighter that I could burn the tips of my fingers on. It smelt of sex, too; of long dead orgasms that shuddered their way from 1967 into the mid 1970s, their last vibrations almost too faint to feel.

He bought a Zodiac next, and I do believe that it was because I so loved the letter Z. Dad told me that I couldn't even see above the dashboard to tell him where we were going. I couldn't be his little navigator in that car, he said. And I've turned and turned those words of his in my mind ever since, wondering whether he thought that if he put me on cushions, or if he switched the Zodiac for the Zephyr, that I'd be able to see; that I'd be his little navigator.

Don't you think I've wished that I'd been there that day? Don't you think I've wished I could have navigated them away from their tragedy? Don't you think I could have done it? I don't know why they went out that day without me, since they always took me everywhere. People spare the feelings of a child, so I was only told that my Mummy and Daddy had 'gone away'. For a long time I thought they should have told me they would go away, should have known that I would not be able to see where they went. But deep in the seeing pit of my guts I knew, so that when, tuned-in by the word Màiri, I heard one of the boys at school telling another, in whispered excitement:

'You couldn't even tell it was a car.'

It felt like an affirmation, a relief. Like throwing-up. Most days I wish I'd been in there with them.

I used to smile unthinkingly when I was a child, a smile coming to my face as irresistibly as my shoulders turn my neck to turn my face to turn my eyes to face a voice. It was less what you'd call a feeling, more a response. Now I'm more careful with my smile. Now it's a matter of composure, and isn't composure everything? I treat my smile as a calculation for others to work out.

Because I killed Alex, and because I saw him so clearly in my mind's eye, I see him still. This does not mean I think he is still alive. I can no longer taste the salt skin of his chest, or feel his raw chin or smell his walnut balls as I'd squeeze him in my hand. Those Alexes I have cast away. I cannot listen to his lies; he does not talk to me from where he is now. He sings to me still, a little, when I'm on his side of the bed.

He was unlucky; he knows that now. All the deceits he played on me he'd played on others, and because they could see they didn't notice. He loved me, that I know to be true, not only because he never said so, not only because of all the things he never did for me, but through his neediness, through the transparency of his hope. He didn't want to lose me, I was the one thing he thought he'd have forever, but I had to punish him; I had to make him leave.

I see Alex now, adjusting his dead feet to avoid me walking into him. Poor Alex, not knowing that I can take anything but betrayal. I can take beating and spitting and looks and pity and fucking with strangers, but not lies. I can even take shoelaces as they fall away from each other, with their little collars of plastic at each end, drumming along the floor. Tap bloody tap. Trip.

Did he tell me he loved me? Did he have to say that? I'd never, ever have asked him, never for a moment invited the suggestion of a response. I liked the way he sent me out to earn my keep, the way he showed me how much I was worth. It was more than I expected, less than he wanted. I liked that, too. He did fall in love with me, I know. I felt that as certainly as a broken bone. It was a different pain, more dramatic and less useful than what had gone before. In one touch, one look (yes, I knew his look), one word Alex made a cage for us both. He could come and go as he pleased, but once made that cage could not be unmade for me. Not even when he washed their smell from him, not even when he brought me lilies, with their visible smell of death. Not when he brought me the voice of Billie Holiday with her help me/leave me cry captured and hammered forever into the smooth surface of a plastic disc. He shouldn't have lined my cage.

People don't blame him for leaving me. That's why I won't get caught; why I haven't even been interviewed, why no-one seems to have noticed his absence, except for me, the one who cannot see. They think it was good of him to stay for so long, gracing me with his absences and his unexplained returns, allowing me his laugh when I asked where he'd been; granting me his company in the places he would take me and roughly forbidding me the places where he wanted to be seen. Gifting me the presence of all the other women he fucked.

Do you want to know how I killed him? Shall I count the ways? I could have rubbed him with salt and had him sweat out the sourness of his life like an aubergine. I could have put him in the freezer, like a side of beef, to await warmth. I could have taken him to the edge of a cliff and had him trip over my ankle so that I could see him fly while he saw himself fall. I could have drowned him in my surplus tears.

But I did none of these things. I killed him here in this church. Does killing people in churches count as more of a sin than killing them anywhere else? Sitting here just now it feels as if it should. But so many have died in churches, locked inside, setalight. Died for their beliefs or lack of them. How I'd love to blaze.

I brought the girls here last week, into the church and down into the unlit tunnels that run north and south beneath the transept and beyond, under the town's streets. These were places of refuge centuries ago. The people of the town would live here during siege and plague, the lucky few. Now these tunnels lie a hundred feet under Sainsbury's and the leisure centre. The smell down in the tunnels is of old sacks, of long-dried grapes, of burnt animals and of liquid cold injected deep into the muscle of living things.

105

The noise of the shopping trolleys does not drift down through the marble floor or permeate the rock and the graves and the dripping wet arched brick roof of the tunnels, not even to my ears. The tight click of badminton rackets on the tiled floor of the sports centre, the leaking shower head in the men's changing room, the sour smell of sweat-filled socks; all these offerings float up to *Ursa Minor,* not down to where life is buried.

They were too excited, down in the darkness, like happy babies at a funeral. They like fear, the girls. They took me to Blackpool in the winter, to the roller coaster. The sea air and the rum and coke kept me sharp, so that I clenched my buttocks as the cogs caught the chain that tugged our car up the long rise. So that I started screaming long before we began our long sweep down and up, down and up and round the tracks. So that I screamed long after the others had stopped.

The tunnels leading from the crypt were my Blackpool for the girls, and I did not let them bring a torch.

'Come down, come down,' I said.

'I'm not following you, you evil bitch,' said Tara. She knew that I liked her calling me a bitch, though no-one else.

'Lead the way yourself,' I said, but they couldn't see and I could.

They ran their hands along the dripping, slimy walls and made retching noises with their throats. They screamed as, carefully late, I told them about the step down. I was making them happy.

Then I heard the rattle of wood over empty space. In all my wanderings I'd never heard it before. One of the girls had stepped on a heavy wooden cover. I'm the dangerous woman, and so we pulled the cover aside and found some stuff to drop down into the void below. Two pence pieces, a lighter, Tara's keys. She was cross about them, said she'd jump in after them, but she didn't. We could hear how big the drop was. Such a long silence and finally a sound like a 3 a.m. drip into an undrained bath. It was a sign-off call. Plop.

I went back the next day and felt like the guilty must feel when they return again and again to the scene of their crime, waiting to be caught. Except in this case there had been no crime, only the impression of one. I walked confidently to the edge of the well, stopping as my toes came to its edge, and knelt beside it carefully. Coin after coin I dropped into it. Five pence pieces at first, but soon it was fifty pences, then lipsticks (my curse), my purse, my mobile phone. Each one signing off. I ran my hand around the inside of the well to make sure it was wide enough to take a man.

'Alex. Alex, do you trust me?'

'I trust you. Yeah.'

'How much?'

'Fuck off.'

'How much do you trust me?'

'What do you want?'

'I want you to play a game. A scary game.'

'Scary?'

'Are you feeling brave?' I could feel the interest rising in him, like the way his cock would swell and throb and demand attention if I put the palm of my hand over the front of his jeans, just so. Whether it wanted to or not. Plop.

'Yeah, I'm feeling brave.'

He was smiling. I could feel his smile, white and wide and winning, but I'll never see it now.

'Come to church with me.'

'Oh, fuck off.'

'We're not going there to pray, Alex. We're going to see the dungeons.'

He liked dungeons.

'We're going to see how good I am in the dark.'

He already knew. He was shaking as we went through the wooden door into the crypt and out the other end into the unlit tunnel.

'I've only got five minutes, Màiri. I'm seeing Jackie at six.'

'Five minutes.'

Alex's hand was sweaty in mine as we stepped towards the gaping mouth of the well and I thought that he might grip hard as he stumbled into its void, dragging us both in, and I thought that would have been fine. But he trod lightly into nothingness; I felt his body shudder, as I'd felt it shudder so often before. The sweat helped his hand to slip easily from mine. I rubbed the soft tip of my thumb across my hand after he said 'Aaaahhhh'. I listened to the slide of his hard, smooth, warm body as it slid fast between the hard, smooth, cold walls of the shaft of the well. I sniffed the fear suddenly mute on my palm and thought of the cartoons Alex watched in the afternoon: 'Aaaahhh,' they said. Once, when I heard him laugh, I asked him to tell me the cartoon's story, but he said it was not worth it.

Plop.

I walked up from the tunnels, through the crypt, up the steps, back through the heavy door, causing the few people in the church to turn and look. A blind woman in the street, in daylight, is an impediment, to herself, to others. She should have a dog, or a man or a stick or dark glasses or something to tell. At night she has her uses, for everyone has their uses at night. But a blind woman in a church has business to attend to. Here everyone can see that she is about the work of God, and the work of God is vengeance.

Mazes

Linda E Clopton

My mother killed herself when I was nine. When they told me, I remembered her in the garden the day before – still as marble with her fingers hooked together as though they might pull apart unbidden. Then she took a step back and folded her arms tightly beneath her breasts. When they told me, I imagined her at the edge of a cliff and stepping back one pace too far, disappearing with arms still folded, wrapped in herself.

"So much to live for." The gossips hovered in flocks as though children couldn't hear stage whispers or couldn't hear at all. So much to live for. But she didn't. The child that was me thought I wasn't good enough, smart enough, or she would have stayed. Now I know it had nothing to do with me. But of course it did. And does. I have danced around death ever since, fascinated as the light-crazed moth.

This brings me to visit Aimee, I suppose, because we've never been close friends. I don't even like her very much. Yet here I am, in spite of three wrong turns. I get lost every time I come. Avoidance, my husband says, ignoring my lousy sense of direction. Today I came on impulse. Another attempt, perhaps, to defy the life inside me, like the soda and onion rings I stopped for on the way. Jim thinks we have waited too late to start a family and worries at my lack of discipline. It's true that I'm not careful, indulging all my junk-food cravings. A subconscious wish for a miscarriage, he says. Abortion by cholesterol? To mitigate my sin, I have brought a cold drink for Aimee. And another for myself. It's a very hot day.

I don't know if Aimee finds my visits painful or stimulating, but she hasn't said *not* to come, and she would if that's what she wanted. Direct, that's Aimee. Unlike this building she lives in, which is a model of digression, a puzzle of hallways and lobbies and anterooms, and anterooms to anterooms, all rendered silent by plush carpeting and Thermopane windows as though sound deprivation might comfort the ill. Enormous potted plants soften the corners but trick the unwary.

I stand a moment trying to get my bearings while my fingers grow numb around the cans of soda. Three corridors lead off from this lobby — is it right and then left, or the other way around? I suspect the floor plan is a pentagon, designed to confuse the grimmest enemy instead of the anxious visitor.

Cuddling the soft drinks, I begin threading my way. I survive two wrong turns and arrive in the lobby where Aimee waits. It's cold here, twenty degrees cooler than outside, and I shiver inside my cotton sun-dress. Extremes have never been easy for me to deal with.

Aimee half reclines in an odd-looking chair on wheels. It reminds me of the chaise longues so beloved by ladies in English novels, but this one has a practical air. Blue vinyl instead of silk brocade. As usual, she is the first to speak, and her greeting racks me with guilt.

"Tomorrow is my birthday," she says. Perhaps I can be excused for not having known this. I can see she doesn't intend to blame.

"I'll be thirty-four. Isn't that incredible?" She looks at me, eyes wide. She doesn't add "... to be thirty-four and dying," but the words float between us like a pesticide fog.

Mother was thirty-five. Ten years earlier, the year after she married, she planted a hedge maze in the field behind our house. It covered half an acre. She copied it from a book on English gardens, and somewhere along the way it changed from hobby to obsession. By the time I was old enough to play there, the walls of holly, glossy and sharp, blocked the world from view.

The maze became a local phenomenon. Presbyterians liked to walk it on Sunday afternoons, and at one point the mayor wanted to put up a billboard. Daddy said no, town folk were welcome, but he refused to become a tourist attraction.

Even so, it made our town unique. Couples courted along the labyrinthine paths, and old men came to advise Mother on how to trim the hedges, what to plant along the narrow verge. She listened, not quite looking them in the eye.

"Try a ground cover, Mrs. Pell. A good perennial like lemon balm spreads without taking over. No trouble."

"I'll give it careful consideration, Mr. Todd," she murmured, hugging herself as they talked. And when he was out of earshot, "There are no perennials," she said softly, stepping backward. "Nothing lives past its season."

What she planted was white, always white, as though color might stain. The paths wandered through snowdrops, anemones, alyssum — and white impatiens she wintered over in jars that lined our dining room windows in parade formation. Their leaves filtered the sun to a green-blue light. "We dine underwater from October to May," Daddy liked to tell visitors.

Mother wore gloves when she gardened, and a wide-brimmed hat that hid her face. She worked with fevered discipline, stopping only to count. How she loved to count! Plants per row, plants not yet in bud, those past blooming. And the maze obeyed her zeal, every inch of it precise as grammar, from its crew-cut hedges to the walkways paved with pebbles smooth as grapes.

Those borders of white offered delicacy and a soothing innocence, but it was the inner circle that drew people onward: an oasis of close-clipped grass with two benches, facing. In late spring the benches nestled amid a riot of tall trumpet-like flowers in pink and coral and red that I learned were amaryllis. The demure border plants flowed up to them, surged around them, seemed to leap upward in a spume of flamboyance. Later, when the holly hedge bore its fruit, I imagined the amaryllis whirling in wild pirouettes, flinging their color in spatters around the walls.

As a child I believed someone had slipped in behind Mother's back to plant that center chamber. Now I wonder what fissure in her hidden self gave vent to that one vivid hurrah. So much to live for.

The colors surrounding Aimee are mostly earth tones, tastefully executed but not exciting. A decor to match lowered voices. A place to tread gingerly.

Someone official walks through and smiles the inevitable smile. "Are

111

you her sister?" she asks *sotto voce*. I smile back. I've lost track of the number of people who have asked this in spite of the total lack of resemblance between Aimee and me, as though they might make me into someone more expedient, someone who belongs.

"Just a friend," I reply as always, but the question raises one of my own. Why hasn't her sister come? A family feud? I doubt if Aimee either grants or accepts forgiveness easily. Then again, it may be a case of fragile sensibilities. Not everyone wants to look for answers.

On my first visit I was too appalled to say the obvious, so Aimee said it for me. "Shocking, isn't it?" She framed her wasted face with her hands as she spoke. A paisley scarf had replaced her luxuriant hair, but those Gypsy eyes remained the same, and she still had remarkably even, white teeth.

"Look at my legs," she said, drawing her gown up above her knees. "I've always wanted beautiful legs. Aren't they sexy?"

In all the years I've known Aimee she has been a generous woman in size, especially from the waist down, but in six months she has changed from Rubens to Erte. Shapely legs. How cruel for circumstances to bestow something desirable when it's no longer useful.

My mother was a desirable woman. I can see that from the photographs we saved — pictures of a slender blonde with a tentative smile that must have sent men scrambling for their shining armor. On her good days she let me help with the maze by assigning me a small task. I liked kneeling next to her, trying to copy what she did with her hands. The pebbles made a pattern on my knees. "Garden kisses," she called them. She would count the pink almond shapes and give me a penny for each one.

Too often, however, Mother walked the paths deep in study, holding herself together with folded arms. Where I saw borders of white, she counted each bedding plant in painful particularity, adding their sum to her list as we meandered, so that we rarely finished the maze until dusk. Even then she wanted to turn back, unsure of her accuracy, until the pangs of hunger out-weighed that other appetite.

Uncertainty does not plague Aimee. She has always known what she wanted and assumed the world must have it to give. She used to infuriate people at neighborhood meetings, so sure she's right and not afraid to speak out, but it worked more often than not. We got our speed bumps.

On my second visit here she talked with a semblance of that old opinionated verve, mostly about people she admires. And about people she loathes. Equal time. Between coughs she chattered on about going to a summer political conference in another state, a sort of camp for lobbyists. Not likely, I thought but didn't say, and if she read the doubt in my face, she ignored it. Living. Making plans.

Today she is subdued, but her gaze impales me so I can't look away. "The doctors have given up on me," she says.

Ah. I don't know how to respond and so keep silent, watching her, wary. Much of conversation depends on rehashing duties fulfilled — shopping, car repairs, busywork. Aimee isn't busy anymore. I lift my Coke and feel the liquid shift. A tiny weight. Her ginger ale sits on the table by her chair. She has opened it but has not drunk. I imagine the carbon dioxide rising from the can and expanding to fill the lounge, choking us both.

At last she begins to speak of inconsequential things. She doesn't ask about Jim, which throws me off guard because she's always been voracious for personal news. Perhaps time is too precious now for either manners or gossip. She is halfway through the plot before I remember that she never used to watch daytime television.

She finishes the soap opera reprise. I sip my drink. I start to tell her about the baby, making it a joke. "At my age! Just when I was ready to run for president."

Her laugh turns into a coughing fit, racking, gargling sounds that leave me inept. She's too fragile to beat on the back. Do something! Do something! I half rise, poised to summon help, when she gags into a handkerchief and leans back in silence.

When able to speak, she does so carefully, not trusting her performance. "My whole life is spent struggling for a clear passage of air," she says.

I ease back onto the edge of my chair and look at the can of soda. A thin, little-girl voice comes out of me. "Would you like some ginger ale?" it asks.

Aimee shuts her eyes.

"Water?"

She shakes her head. We sit quietly for a moment, breathing.

"It's really hot for June." Now my voice erupts in raucous decibels. "The radio said middle nineties."

Aimee breathes.

"School lets out next week. The neighbors' kids will be on the loose again."

Aimee opens her eyes.

"It's too soon," I say with a laugh. "I'm not ready."

Aimee looks at me. She takes another breath. "Camp," she says.

I grab for the word, hold on to it for ballast. "Camp. Yes. They'll be going to summer camp."

A young man in a wheelchair comes into the lounge and Aimee gathers her energy. "Hey there. I thought you'd left."

He grins. "Couldn't stay away from you," he says.

She tosses her head. The ends of the paisley scarf swing like curls. "Are you coming to my birthday party tomorrow?"

It shocks me that she's flirting although I'm not sure why. The dying should be above carnal pleasures? Think only of spiritual things?

Discreetly, and because the Coke has gone straight through, I rise and cross to the Ladies' room. It's very clean; the disinfectant is only mildly annoying. I linger, giving Aimee and her young man privacy for their futile mating dance, wondering if she has adjusted her robe to show off her legs.

In the lavatory mirror my face looks back at me with a light blush but not because of the much-touted glow of pregnancy. The lighting here flatters the skin. Like all of the public-space decor, it perpetuates the myth of eternal health. The deity, Health. Youth is only a secondary god.

Automatically, I look for wrinkles. Not many; not bad. I turn sideways. My belly strains against my loose sun-dress, impatient with camouflage. I am several years older than Aimee yet my womb is still fruitful, while hers is killing her. There are no perennials.

For weeks after Mother's death I went to the maze. Each time I thought I knew the way. So I dawdled, lay stomach down on the benches to feel sun on my back, drew patterns in the gravel and smoothed them out again, listened to bees court the amaryllis. But if twilight came before I reached the puzzle's end, the gorge of panic began to rise in my throat. I listened for footsteps but heard none; fancied there was laughter from the house across the field. There is solace in solitude. No balm at all in being left behind.

I trudged along each path, grinding my teeth in the effort not to call out, afraid my voice would tremble if I did. The razor-leafed hedge turned from green to gray to black. Pebbles lost their shape. And when at last Daddy called from near at hand, his voice anxious, I stumbled toward its compass point and ran into the open too numb to weep. Behind me the maze closed its arms and waited for someone else to count its secrets, to look for promised peace in its retreat.

Do we all in the end step back in surrender? Fold ourselves with relief into the final womb? If so, then what does it matter whether we take our own life or leave it to some outside force to choose time and place and means?

I taste a hint of bile, the soft drink's epitaph. In the rest room mirror my eyes stare back at me, solemn with unanswered questions. I fold my arms beneath my breasts. My image does the same. Unfolding, I extend both hands until palms meet mirrored palms. Stalemate. When the glass becomes warm beneath my touch, I step back, leaving ghostly handprints that immediately start to fade.

I walk out of the rest room and find the lobby vacant. It's so quiet I feel I've stepped into a time warp. Aimee is gone. Vanished. The can of ginger ale still sits on the end table, its bright green accenting the restful taupe and mushroom decor as though put there by an interior designer.

For another moment I stand at a loss. I feel the baby move, perhaps in protest. The onion rings are crowding us both. In the hallway a nurse's aide pushes an old man past the door and I remember: Aimee's chair had wheels. She has not been taken up in a flash like Elijah.

Faint wheel tracks crisscross the carpet in a tic tac toe game not yet played. The deepest tracks lead to the corridor on the left. I hesitate.

115

Surely that isn't the way to Aimee's room. The young man's perhaps. He was propelling himself, but Aimee is too weak to jockey her chair more than a few feet and far too weak for a tryst.

I find the nurses' station and follow their directions. The hallway tile unwinds in a smooth artery with seams invisible to normal sight. It's a special kind, designed to take the punishment of many wheels and soles without showing wear. Durable.

In her room Aimee still sits in the blue chair. A vase on a table holds three bright peonies. Two of the blooms are nearly spent, but no one has discarded them. The third quivers with vitality. It faces away from the others in glorious denial.

An aide hovers, intent on getting her charge back into bed, and her diligence reminds me of my own schedule. I am car pool chauffeur this week for school children on our block, racking up points for future favors. The final bell will ring now before I arrive, releasing them to stumble down the steps, clumsy with laughter.

Conversation turns more awkward than before, both of us thinking of time. I mentally retrace my steps, calculating how long it will take to find my way through halls and anterooms and lobbies to the exit nearest my car, knowing I must allow myself the wrong turns I'll make.

Aimee does most of the talking now. She takes a long pause, conserving her energy, yet devours my face even in silence. But five children wait in front of the school; five mothers wait at home. And I don't belong here.

I give Aimee a quick kiss the way friends greet, or part, on social occasions. She holds out her arms and I slip my hands down them gently, slowly, feeling her pulse against my own. I leave, aware of her eyes. But as I call a cheerful good-bye, I know what I'll remember: her arms stretched out toward life as it drew away.

Locked Down

Sophie Spalding

Her labour began, finally, nine drawn-out days past due. Ciaran was finishing up his last pint, wondering what might be on the box later when his mobile rang. He hadn't been clear until quite late in her pregnancy that the drive to Holles Street and all that went with it would actually be required of him. Still, once this message had been delivered and received, he'd resigned himself to whatever had to be done.

According to the clock above the admissions desk, they'd checked in just after half two. Things got a bit hairy at a few points in the following six hours. But, while he was aware she might not look on things this way, he reckoned she didn't have it half bad for a first baby. She'd been clear from the outset about her attitude towards giving birth; 'Knock me out and wake me up when the hairdresser leaves,' she liked to joke. This was all new to Ciaran. He thought today's women were into empowerment, birthing pools, hours of swapping horror stories about botched episiotomies and forceps-happy obstetricians. Either way, by four fifteen she was five centimetres dilated, epidural up and running and at eight thirty-four a.m. the midwife was cutting the cord, pronouncing their son's arrival.

She was given a few minutes with the baby. He wormed about on her front while she did the laugh-blubber thing, her tears steering a wide course around her smile. She kept kissing him, stroking his shock of sticky black hair, telling him he was beautiful. Ciaran thought he should do something so he reached over, laid a hand on the gunk-covered back. He'd wondered how he'd be at this moment, worried he might come across as switched off, bored. What he actually felt was a familiar swelling in his chest, behind his eyes a stinging. She placed her hand on top of

117

his, said 'thanks' in that little voice of hers he would never get used to. He brushed her clammy forehead with his lips, whispered, 'Well done mum' and for a moment he imagined they looked like any other couple in the hospital that morning.

While she was being seen to, the nurses scooped baby into a towel and took him off to be poked, prodded and dressed. He gave her hand a squeeze, gestured towards the pale blue uniforms, traipsed behind them to the other side of the room, where he stood swaying with tiredness and trying to look involved till one of them suggested he grab his chances to sit, pointed to an orange plastic chair in the corner.

'Daddy would like to hold his son now?' The tiny Philippine nurse, who'd been wrapped heroically round one of her legs towards the end of the delivery. 'Good, Daddy,' she cooed, tucking the swaddled child into the crook of his arm, 'you are a natural.' He peered into the solemn face. He'd always loved brand new babies. There was something about them, the way they didn't entirely belong to this planet, and this one was a real spacer; one of those silent, star-gazers, blurry, unblinking eyes meandering around the room, halting here and there, mesmerised by who knows what. For a while he seemed to stare straight at Ciaran. Did he remind him of anyone? The hair could be Sorcha when she was born but he was never any good at seeing people in babies. This used drive Una round the twist. 'Look,' she'd insist, 'for godsake look at the way she yawns. It's exactly like my dad.' Una had it all down; it was obvious for anyone to see that Sorcha was the spitting image of his mother, Aine the walking reincarnation of her father.

The big, curly-headed nurse approached, the one who'd been ordering her to push, not to push, to blow the candles out, to pant, to push again while the other one went on about how well she was doing. Nurse bad cop waved a tiny plastic identity bracelet at him. 'Have ye a name picked?' Ciaran hadn't anticipated this. His eyes shot across the room hoping she might pipe up, bale him out. Her head lolled in his direction, eyes fixed on the baby, as if to compensate for the recently severed umbilical connection. But she was either too spaced out or far off to catch what was being said down his end of the room.

'Eh, we haven't decided yet.' Ciaran thought he sounded like a snared

118

child snatcher.

'We'll put down Baby Roche so, will we?' She made meaningful eye contact with him, nodding her head up and down, which led him to nod back, thus settling that one in what he hoped was a satisfactory manner.

Of course coming up with a name was entirely her bag. Once or twice he'd joked how no boy should be called after him. Otherwise, he'd said nothing. Una had always preferred to do the naming after the child was born, said she had to meet them first. Back when Sorcha was on the way, he'd once mentioned he liked the name Shane. But the boy next door to Una growing up had been a Shane and he was a little git, on top of which he'd had the world's most wicked buck teeth.

She was wheeled up to her room, him keeping pace, the child in his arms, trying not to tangle with trolley wheels, bump elbows with nurses and orderlies. She was dying to hold the baby. 'Hello little man,' she said, stroking his hands, his downy cheeks. He was starting to ponder the question of how soon he might be able to split. Her mother'd be in soon. All her mates would be lined up around the block. He reckoned he wouldn't have to show again till tomorrow night and with any luck she'd be out Tuesday. Of course, Wednesday would be one to miss. He was running through the list of her friends, wondering who could be roped in to do the honours for Day Three when a nice Scottish nurse came to do the breastfeeding spiel. In another stroke of fortune he wasn't entirely sure she grasped, junior proved himself an obliging and efficient fellow in this department. One sniff of a tit set him reaching with his hungry fledgling mouth. He thought of Una with Sorcha, up half the night trying to get her to latch on, her nipples cracked and raw, weeping a sickly mix of colostrum and blood.

She winced, shifted off one of her hips. 'You haven't taken any pictures.' She sounded narky, was probably starting to head down. And she looked shattered, like she'd been exploded from the inside out, her hair plastered to her head, snail trails of salt and spit running ragged lines across her blotchy face. A smear of brownish-orange, iodine or something, streaked over her jaw. Her hospital gown hung open, an over ripe, danish blue breast perched on top of her stomach. She was used to dolling herself up, looking her best. He thought he'd better focus on the

119

baby. He rooted in her bag, dug out the camera, snapped a few shots, trying to remember any tips on photography. Next she wanted her mobile; speed dialled her mother. He disappeared into the corridor, to give her a bit of privacy, also in hopes of finally locating a smoking area.

For the third time since they'd arrived at the hospital, he ended up standing on a toilet, puffing like a schoolboy out a fly window in the gents. She was still on the phone when he got back, googling over the baby, how gorgeous he was. Even on to the gories of her labour, she was smiling and animated. 'He comes at me with this huge needle, tells me to arch my back like a cat, not move a muscle. This in the middle of a massive contraction.' He was pleased for her then, even foolishly proud of himself. He'd given her what she wanted. Also, the better she felt, the greater his chances of escape. A nurse came to check on her. 'I've to go now, Mum,' she said, 'they need to do something. See you after lunch and, listen, don't forget the vests and the bottled water.'

'Didn't anyone tell you?' the nurse asked.

'What?'

'The winter vomiting bug,' she said. Ciaran's mind went to work on the concept of winter. It was the twentieth of September. Everyone was going around talking about Indian summer.

'As of this afternoon, this hospital's completely locked down. Only partners are allowed visit for at least the rest of the week.'

'I'm talking about my mother. He's her first grandchild.'

'Sorry love, partners only. We have to insist. You'll be out before you know it. Meanwhile, thank god for those yokes, eh?' she gestured towards the mobile, 'Oh, and them too, I suppose.' She waved her thermometer in Ciaran's direction, smiling as she left.

'I don't believe it,' she wailed, her eyes filling again. In meaner moments, he had thought that she was an exceptionally unattractive crier. Una could bawl for hours, walk into the bathroom, splash some water on her face and look positively bright-eyed. She couldn't seem to shed a tear or two without puffing up and getting bloodshot. She'd been only the most practised smiles when they'd met, not that he'd been any more than dimly aware of her when she'd sat beside him on the plane.

'They're fine, absolutely fine,' Una kept saying the whole five days he was over. Of course they talked about him, she assured him, but it seemed they didn't miss him at all. Apparently he was supposed to greet this news with relief. 'Well thank god for that! Thank god my children can take off to live in England, plonk a picture of me on their bedside lockers and not look back!' Apparently, also, they were both to forget, ignore completely, all the admissions she'd extracted from him over the years. He was to draw no comparisons, see no possible similarity between how they might feel and his troubles over his own absentee father.

At his absolute worst that first visit, he'd sulked continuously round Una; made her repeat everything at least three times just for spite – 'Huh', 'Sorry, What'd you say?' – disappeared at the drop of a hat, even going awol in the middle of a trip to a pizza restaurant that was supposed to be his treat. He was fine when it was just the girls but once Una was there he could think of nothing but how to get up her nose. Each day he'd wake aching on her couch, listen to the girls fight over breakfast cereal in their wet-week English accents and feel all his late night reason and resolve vanish into the wincing morning light.

They were still fine apparently as they waved him off with the ludicrously overpriced lollipops he'd bought them in the airport shop. Three pound sterling each for a bog-standard lolly on a plastic stick shaped like a dinosaur. He'd have paid ten times that not to have to watch them standing there sucking so desperately on their dinopops. Una tried to shunt them on their way but they'd refused to budge, kept standing there the whole time he went through security. The steel caps in his Cats had set the beeper off and he'd taken ages. In the middle of trying to unlace his boots, yank them off, then pull them back on again, reminding himself all the while not to forget his wallet, his phone and his keys in the little plastic dish, his carry-on bag on the conveyer belt, he'd kept having to turn back around and wave again. 'Byee, bye-byee!' Even Una was chewing her lip. He'd headed straight for the bar, started with a double and was half jarred before they'd called his flight.

They were somewhere over the Irish Sea and he'd just cracked his third tin of Carlsberg when she spoke. 'Are you by any chance a nervous flyer?' In equal parts cheek and sympathy, she pointed out he'd been plastered to his head-rest, his right foot drumming a hummingbird beat since take off. He always found it easier to talk when he'd drink taken and was he ever in need of distraction. He told her he couldn't understand how planes stayed up in the air, how each time he landed he thought he'd experienced a genuine miracle, the rest of his life stretching before him like some eleventh-hour reprieve from death row. He'd surprised himself how amusing he sounded and she'd giggled obligingly, explained she flew on a weekly basis with her job. She was an accounts manager, she said, for an ad agency. It wasn't half as glamorous as it sounded. She'd been sent to London last minute this morning, come straight to the airport from a long and very liquid lunch. They didn't quite manage the mile high club on the last fifteen minutes of the Stansted to Dublin but she'd offered to hold his hand during landing and he'd returned the favour by insisting on seeing her to her car. They'd started kissing the face off each other in the short-term car park. From there it was into her 02 Freelander and straight to her apartment in Smithfield.

He'd had to pinch himself when he'd woken in her place next morning, all the more so when she turned round and hopped on him again. But that was nine months ago and light years from the bewildering nativity scene unfolding around him. He shuffled past the baby, now sleeping in his Perspex crib, handed her a wodge of tissues. It was hard for him to have any idea how he really felt about this woman, what it might have been like to meet under different circumstances. There were two versions of events. Hers was the old-fashioned one; two very drunk people, two recently separated people, one very crazy night. For the first while he'd wandered around believing just this. Then Una rang late one Friday. Her sister had been over. They'd been drinking red wine. Una was never good with red wine. After Claire went home, she'd started sorting her CDs and old LPs from their packing boxes, dug out Glenn Campbell. Somewhere in the middle of 'By the time I get to Phoenix' she'd dialled his number. For the first time since it had dawned on him she was serious about leaving, he had her with a chink in her armour. They talked for a while, Una crying softly, Ciaran basking in her guilt. He reckoned sooner or later she'd get wind of his 'situation' and it seemed as good a time as any to spill the beans. Of course that was it for the warm and fuzzies. After demanding to know the details – 'You think this doesn't concern me?' –

she'd hung up on him, must have got straight onto LiveLine or something and it turned out (naturally!) that someone's friend had a sister who knew her since college. In less than forty-eight hours, he was being given the low-down on what a fool he'd been taken for, how her ex had refused to have kids, how people he'd never even met were going around calling her 'the raider', him 'the donor'.

He badly needed to get going, now, cleared his throat, checked his watch again. Ten forty-seven.

'Don't go yet, please.'

'Look, I'll come in every visiting,' he offered, forcing up the corners of his mouth in what he hoped might pass as a reassuring smile. 'I'll ring Shay; explain the situation. He'll get one of the lads to cover for me till you're out.' She cried even harder then and he honestly couldn't tell was it gratitude or disgust at the prospect of him as her sole visitor.

But then he'd spent a lot of time in the past nine months not knowing what to say while women cried. Una had taken the pregnancy surprisingly badly. Her initial anger he'd expected; not what came after. Once his news had sunk in fully, it seemed as if all her trademark grit and resolve abandoned her. Before he'd told her, he might have believed he'd find some vengeful pleasure in her suffering. And, if he were perfectly honest, he did enjoy the odd five minutes of pure pay-back. But he'd seen her nurse her mother through end-stage cancer, juggling two kids and a part-time job. He'd been worse than useless to her then, hanging around drinking all hours, signing up for extra shifts. Anything rather than go home. And yet she'd stayed standing. It had to be said, their whole relationship (post relationship?) was based on the premise that Una was in charge, at least of herself and, by extension, the girls. Ciaran knew he needed her this way.

The Friday after his news broke, she'd picked him up at the airport minus the girls. They'd gone to school after all. It was important, she said, as new girls, they didn't stand out from the crowd, miss too many days. They'd gone straight to her house and had hours of the most wrenching sex, the kind you could only have with someone you've known forever, the kind you might have when someone dies or something, the kind he wished now they could have had after her mother. Even he'd done some

123

crying and at one stage he'd found himself the astonished recipient of a tantrum-style pummelling, Una hammering at his shoulders with balled up fists, 'You're MY Ciaran. You're MY Ciaran.'

They'd both gone on the school run, still dazed, grazed, touching, the girls making faces at each other in the back of the car. But by the time she'd got them down that night she'd veered back to angry. He was in the front room, half-heartedly flicking the channels, thinking how odd and ridiculous it was that he felt different watching the BBC in England. She grabbed the zapper, snapped the telly off.

'So, how many more little half-brothers and sisters are we likely to hear about? Of course they'd both assumed Una would be first to 'meet someone else', with all the fortification and protective padding that offers. She was hands-down the more attractive prospect – she was starting the new life, in a new country, with the new job, the instant circle of nice English friends courtesy of her sister. She'd always been the socialiser, the joiner, and there was nothing wrong with Una to look at. It stood to reason sooner rather than later she'd catch someone's eye. Oh, he would have done his bit acting the bollocks about it, but he was good at that. She wasn't. As if she'd been home all the time in her apron, waiting while his dinner went cold, she'd accused him of everything under the sun; he was a heartless philanderer; couldn't keep his dick in his pocket; hadn't bothered to consider the consequences of his actions for the girls.

He could think of a few comebacks and counter-arguments but mostly he just let it all wash over him. For one thing, Ciaran had a natural tolerance, an empathy with anyone in circumstances such as Una's. He knew what it was like to feel you'd to hold a certain line even if this meant the blatant rejigging of history. And eight years of marriage had taught him to sit through detailed analyses of his failures and shortcomings. In fact, he'd even invented his own little word game involving the lyrics of his favourite Talking Heads songs for just such occasions. 'Oh Please! Not the one about going out on your own again,' she'd start, to which he'd think,

'This is not my beautiful wife' – Ten words, four or more letters, starting with B: Blah, Blather, Blame, Bemoan, Bane, Bother, Blast, Batter, Beat, Bash. Or,

'Have you ever even heard the words 'financial planning'?'

'Burning down the house'…Shit, Snit, Snot, Snub, Snob, Shout, Shut, Shunt, Shrew, Singe.

But now no sooner would he settle back into the shadow of her judgement than she'd switch to clingy again. For the rest of the pregnancy, she'd been yo-yo woman, ringing up in the middle of the night to declare him a cheating bastard, calling back to apologise. He was to come over right now, sit down, tell the girls what he'd done. No, he was to wait till the baby was born first.

The last time he'd been over they'd stayed up all night talking. She confided that she'd come round to thinking she could just about stand the thoughts of him having a child with this woman as long as it was a girl. She knew it shouldn't matter but the fact that they'd only ever had daughters together made a son sound too special, too different and exclusive to him. She said he could laugh but she'd even had this fantasy in which he and the woman were killed in an car crash and Una and the girls adopt the little half-sister, welcome her into their family, Geldof style.

He tried kidding with her how he only did girls, kept repeating that this woman had no intentions with him. He'd promised to see her through the pregnancy. They were getting together to talk through what to do about the child. But Una had said it herself; she was a sperm raider. She'd her own money, never once suggested he move in, and pregnancy had put her right off sex. The truth was a little more complicated. Sure it would never be worth her while looking for financials from Ciaran. The lie about sex he considered at worst off-white under the circumstances; there hadn't been that much going down, nothing at all for months now and certainly nothing thrilling enough to risk wounding Una any further. But as for her true intentions, mostly he was afraid to ask. What she did say only deepened his confusion. He honestly didn't know what it could mean for him. 'Ciaran,' she had explained, 'this is your baby too. I understand if you choose not to get involved but I want you to know I won't stop you taking up your position as father.'

***

The hall porter pulled open the door and Ciaran shot from the hospital like someone who'd spent the night between floors in a lift. He halted himself

125

instantly, pulled out his pack of Marlboro, stood lighting up in the weak morning sun. A woman passing by gave him a 'look at daddy' smile. He hurried round the corner, anxious to disassociate himself with all things Holles Street.

He was back on the doorstep just four hours later. 'C'mon, c'mon', he growled at the door, a bunch of 'It's a boy' balloons bobbing cheerfully behind him. On his way in he'd spent several excruciatingly awkward minutes standing in her mother's hallway being handed three bottles of Evian, a large carrier bag full of baby clothes and gift packages and, of course, the obligatory helium balloons. Mrs. Roche had borrowed one of those instamatic cameras, which she slung around his neck with orders to take loads of pictures. He could drop them by her house on his way home tonight; pick up any cards and gifts that had been left in for her. He was to make sure she was okay for nighties and whatever else she might need.

The pair of them were out for the count when he got to the room. He lowered himself into the chair at the end of the bed, sat watching his son shudder and sigh in his sleep. It was twenty past three. Visiting ended at five. He wouldn't bother going home between then and seven. He'd find somewhere near to have a quiet pint, wet the poor critter's head by himself. Aside from her mother and sorting things with Shay, he hadn't spoken to a single person. He hadn't the heart to. He knew as soon as he opened his mouth now he was bound to betray someone. He'd switched on his mobile when he'd got back to his car this morning. Up popped his text message from Una, the same one she'd been sending every day for two weeks now, simply reading, 'Wel?' Before he'd started up his engine he'd keyed in his reply. 'Boy. 7.01@8:34am. Ma & Ba fine. Da v v fkd up.' Then he'd powered off again.

Flagged

Janice Nabors Raiteri

"Let 'em through."

"Okay." Stomach in. Head high. Shoulders back. Slow flag over and up. Nice and easy, keep it breezy. Waving with no wind to help me. Whoa, not so close, Miss Swerve to Miss Me Mitsubishi. Move it over. Into the left lane, Mitzu. Don't need your imported engine heat melting my all-American ass.

Wish I hadn't worn any underwear. Started not to, then thought maybe I better, county regulations and all. Like them pencil pushing pansy regulators ever stood on Highway 42 for eight hours straight on the tenth of July. Then again, maybe they have. Could be what's wrong with them, sun done blistered their brains. It's gotta be at least a hundred and twenty. You know that heat index thing. All this traffic on new asphalt. Geez, my boobs itch. Gotta scratch something fierce. Bra's soaked. Wish I could yank it off. Could try that Flashdance thing, you know, the welder-dancer girl. She wiggled outta her bra all the time keeping her sweatshirt on so's nobody'd see nothing. Course, these taxpaying commuters wouldn't notice if I's standing here buck naked. I tell you, I'm out here bustin' my butt trying to be the best damn flag girl in Florida and they sittin' in their cars, eating, talking, practicing karaoke, not thinking of nothing but their own selfish selves. I could jump on this flag and fly right outta here and they'd be saying, "Did you see something funny? Wasn't there a girl over that way holding a flag or something?" Pearls before swine, that's all

"Keep 'em coming, Analee."

"Come on. Slow, slow now." Flag's a flutterin' and it ain't stutterin'.

Sweat's in my eyes, even trickling down my legs. Be a miracle if I

127

make it through one more day out here. I swear to goodness you just never know what kinda hand life's gonna deal you. Fold 'em or hold 'em. Stay or play. In or out. I thought I had me a royal flush with this job, but I'm here to tell you that I'm fixin' to start thinking about maybe gettin' ready to

"Stop 'em, Analee. We gotta pull crossways."

Sure. Whatever you say Mr. Head of the Road Crew looking down from your high and mighty ivory tower air-conditioned truck. I coulda had your job if I hadn't of been a girl and

"Analee!"

"Yes sir!" Circle round the world. Dip. Turn. Flip it over, change the color. Stop side. No more slow. Don't bother honking, you just can't go.

"Show us what you got, Flag Girl!"

Well, Mr. Chevy Camaro. I'll have you know I coulda got paid for showing what I got. In a cool and classy gentleman's club. Went with Tiffany Friday night and she said that they said what with my dancing experience as a flag girl at Harold High, well, I had the rhythm and wouldn't nobody notice I'd never had no ballet 'cept for that one month back at the community center. They'd of hired me right then and there, but I told 'em I wasn't real sure, I sorta was and sorta wasn't. Anyway, didn't see not one gentleman. They's all like you, Camaro Creep. Got the little woman back home trying to fix you a decent dinner on her piddly ass grocery budget cause you done spent it all on booze and broads and bucket seats and whatever else makes your sorry little self feel like a big man. Bet Barby's Dolls woulda paid me more'n you make. Let's see now, you look like a Mr. Johnston type. Department store rooster struttin' round his hen house, hovering over all the women with his hands-on management routine. Four and a half weeks in junior miss dresses was thirty-two days too long for me and besides

"Analee. Let 'em through."

"Uh huh." Over the head, flim-flam, figure eight, then shimmy-sham. Slow now. Go ahead, folks. Suffocate me with your exhaust fumes. Maybe if I'm fightin' for my last breath I'll forget about the heat. Notice me then, I bet. This flag draped over me, laying here deader'n a doornail. Slow, slow. Left lane. Come on, Miss Jeep Grand Cherokee, God's gift to the world college girl all gussied up, spending daddy's money buying that perfect little three hundred dollar dress for the big game. Well, you ain't nothing' I couldn't of been, but I never had no daddy's money cause he blew it all fore he left, just like Camaro Creep on up the road there. I had to pay my own way. Went to Pensacola Tech. I coulda graduated if I'd of wanted to, but good grief, it was "Analee, pick a major! Analee, math or science? Analee, two years or three?" It's a wonder I made it through a whole semester. Nuh unh now, don't you be smiling down at me, Miss Jeep Grand. You look like one of those sorority girls used to come into the diner every Thursday night, ordering me around like I didn't have nothing to do but wait on them, then getting me fired hollerin' about grape soda not coming outta white silk. Fine with me. Six week's bout five too many slinging hash. Pull on through, Miss Jeep Grand. Don't wanna see nothing but your tail lights in the distance.

Slow now. Left lane, folks. Stir up some dust. Anything to make my job more miserable. Hey, hey. Look at the flag. It's flappin' steada yappin'. Left lane, Mrs. Respectable Riviera. Think you too good to pay attention? Think you the only woman live got a husband and children? Well, Mrs. Respectable, I coulda had me a husband if I'd of wanted one. Month with most men's about three weeks too long. I say it's like bass fishing. Catch 'em, then throw 'em back. And don't you be looking at me like you something and I ain't. I know your kind, Mrs. Re. Say you taking care of the kids and scrubbing floors when all the while you're snoopin' on your two-timing husband. I see that smirk on your face. Same smirk Coach Casey's wife smirked whole time she's throwin' a hissy fit, screaming bout getting me kicked off the drill team and all the time knowing I could twirl my flag so fast, be like a optical illusion, seeing the next side fore you ever even seen the first. Not my fault her husband couldn't keep his hands to hisself. Course, she thought it was just a fling, but I'm here to tell you that man really loved me. Only one I ever wanted to keep and damn if he didn't throw his ownself back. We coulda had us a good thing, but it turned out all wrong cause his wife made him do the right thing. She figured he couldn't of been anywhere close to serious 'bout some silly flag girl lived in a double-wide. Bet you got the same problem, Mrs. Respectable, wondering why your husband'd be messin' round with somebody you think you so much better than. Well, Re, you the kind of woman I used to love looking down on from my fifteenth floor desk in catalogue order. Best part of that job. Only worked there for a few weeks, but I can tell you

"Analee! Gonna have to stop them for a good bit while we spread this tar. Let a few more through, then stop 'em. Smile or something. Strut your stuff. Keep 'em happy."

Yeah, I got your happy, like maybe if your pompous pansy ass'd get my paycheck steada yours. Sitting gets salary. Standing's hourly. Reckon what they'd pay me if I fall out flat from a heat stroke? I'm out here frying and you up there cool as a cucumber and bout half as smart.

"Come on through." Wave it gently. Slow side. "Come on!" Give it some gas, Miss Forty Miles to the Gallon. You think you making a statement in that VW bug cause your engine's behind steada front. I remember when all my mama had was an old beat-up beetle. Kids hollering "hippie bug" at us. We wasn't making no statement. Only ride we could buy. Go on now, Miss Brand New Beetle, you gotta go save the world with your herbal tea drinking tree hugging

"Hold 'em back, Analee!"

"Okay." Flip my flag and hold it high. Stand your ground and make 'em sigh. Stop side. No fake. Brake. Stop, folks. That's it. Time for all you back-stabbing, social climbing snobs to get out those itty-bitty cell phones and cancel those great big appointments. Oh my now, won't it be a miracle? You ain't there and life goes right on. Unh uh, don't be rollin' down no windows and yelling at me. Just doing my job like I been doing better'n anybody all summer, but I'm beginning to think that's been about two months too long for

Honk. Honk.

Great. Now I gotta listen to Mr. Jaguar Gigolo laying on his horn. Whatsa matter Jag, couldn't find nothing else to lay on?

"Hey, Honey! How about letting me go around?"

"No sir. Can't. Gotta wait. Won't be long." And I ain't your honey, Jag boy. Had me one like you few years ago. Carl. Moved in with me cause he's between jobs. Course, so was I, but before I could turn around twice, he'd took off with my granddaddy's stamp collection, of all things. My

130

pawpaw's last words were 'Analee, don't you let nothing happen to these stamps. They gonna take care of you long after I'm dead and gone.' Well, how's I supposed to know they's worth anything? Pawpaw never was. Carl went and got hisself a new Jaguar, just like you driving, Mr. Gig. Last I saw him, he wadn't nothing but a blur going

Honk. "Hey, Honey! Come on. Move over. This Jag can cut it round the side."

"No sir. Can't do it." You think those 'Soft Shoulder' signs are for decoration? You wouldn't get fifty feet 'fore your shiny mag wheel's be sinking you sideways. Those scrub bushes just happen to be covering up a right steep drop-off other side of 'em. Old barbed wire fence might catch you, might not. You ever think maybe I'm here for a reason?

Honk. "Hey! Move it, Flag Girl! I can't sit here all day."

"If I can stand here all day, seems to me you could sit." Mr. Big Wig Jag Gig.

"What's the matter? This some kind of power trip for you – making us stay here?"

"No, sir. Just doing my job. Shouldn't be much longer."

Honk. "Move it, Bitch!" Honk. "Let me through. Now!" Honk, honk, honk.

"Well, Sir, since you put it that way." Flip it around, wave him through, then back to stop, no folks, not you. Just Mr. Jag here. He's special. You go right on through, Honey. That's right, scoot over more, on the shoulder.

"Analee! How'd that son of a bitch get through? He'll never make it!"

My, my, all this excitement's got my mind off my misery. Never saw Mr. Head of the Road Crew jump outta that truck so fast. Left the door open, all that cool air driftin' out.

Drop the flag and let it lie, time this flag girl said good-bye.

I can run right past 'em. Nobody'll notice me. Such a commotion. Oops. Looks like Mr. Jag's slipping. Don't always pay to be pushy now does it Jag boy?

Make the jump. Girl, you got flair. Close the door. Feel that cool air. Let's see now. First gear. I'm outta here. Pull away, go into second. Get some speed and up to third. Yes!

131

Oh, dear. Hmm. Let's see now. Straight'll take me down toward Ft. Walton. Could turn right here, head west to Pensacola. Or left, go back over to Harold and pull smack into Coach Casey's driveway. Tell him he ain't never gonna be happy less he stands up for what he wants and sits down right here beside me. But then, what if he won't go? What in tarnation would I do then? Oh, oh, I don't know. Jump 'n Pump's up ahead, could stop and try to figure out ... no, don't want to stop just yet. Down into fourth. South? No, west? No. Yes. Oh, I don't know. Exit one mile. Oh dear. Get off here? Stay on? Okay, Analee, calm down, calm down. Be cool. Okay, yeah, okay. I got it. Turn on the radio. If it's a happy song, I'll go east, straight to Coach Casey. Sad, I'll go west and just keep on going. But then, what'll I do if it's one of those middle of the road sad but kinda happy songs? Or even worse, what if it don't have no words?

The Backroom Rebellion

Rosemary Jenkinson

'Back for another day in jail then,' Uel joked as he passed Gerard's desk.

Gerard laughed. Jail was right enough. Though there were windows in the office there was little natural light because of the fortress walls outside.

He liked Uel, warmed to his humour, though he tried not to. There were no airs with Uel. He was what he was – a kind, big, tatie-bred man. Gerard guessed from his name he was a Protestant. It was harder to make judgements now the Police Service was recruiting so many Catholics. In any case individual religion didn't make a difference to Gerard since all police endorsed the British government and were therefore combatants.

A deep rumble came from the bowels of the water dispenser.

Now that other Constable, John Rainey, was easier to hate. He marched around the office space like a bandsman with his radios at the ready, his bottle-green uniform bulking out his body in the fashion of a provincial robocop. He whistled at the female staff over the intercom and laid the blame on the man at the front desk, the black bastard.

Gerard shared the large office with about twenty other pen-pushers. He'd been there a few weeks and had already been given routine access to documents detailing transfers and sick leave. He delivered the post round private offices in the morning and was gradually getting to know the codes of filing cabinets and computer systems. The trust or laxity of the staff never ceased to amaze him.

He looked up from his forms and wondered if any of his colleagues were the same as him. Sometimes people gave clues to where their sympathies lay. John Rainey talked of 'going to Ireland' like it was a foreign country, like the big hind didn't know he was in Ireland already. The astute ones avoided names and talked of being from 'this part of the world.'

No, he suspected he was not alone. There had to be another sleeper or mole in reserve. The Ra didn't leave things to chance.

Gerard O'Hara was twenty-two. Gerard Patrick Seamus O'Hara-Up-The-IRA he'd used to boast at St Patrick's. His family in Dundrum had never had paramilitary connections. It was only when he'd gone to Queen's and run around with some Sinn Fein members that he'd been put in contact with 'Sean'. Sean said they were looking for young people with clean records, that the war was being waged on a different front. Sean had given him the key to a small bedsit in decent area of East Belfast where no one was likely to drive him out because of his Catholic name. Gerard then waited five weeks for his security clearance before taking up his post in personnel with the police service.

Looking back on it, there wasn't really a definitive moment that had pushed him into the IRA. Martin McGuinness, for instance, hadn't been able to get a job because of his religion but Gerard had never known that kind of discrimination. He remembered the day he'd got on the wrong school bus home and the Protestant kids had started singing the sash at him and throwing conkers, their faces battle-warped. No, but it wasn't that which had made him join. It was the white heat, the frustration of being in this little Unionist statelet, a sense of rebellion that going into politics couldn't satisfy. That and the fear of going up in flames like a suicide bomber without a cause. And deep-down he was glad that the war had changed and he wouldn't be blooded. In principal he believed in violence towards combatants but the reality was he could hardly bear killing a fly. He would always miss with his first shot with a rolled up newspaper and, hearing it fly into a tizz, he regretted causing so much unnecessary fear before its elimination.

'Hi, Mum.'

'How're you keeping, son?'

'Grand. And yourself?'

The conversation would always end with his Mum reminding him that he was just a wee hop away and when was he coming home. He would come up with the excuse that he was too busy and when he put the phone down, he would turn his eyes inward and think of the whitewashed house, its chimney jutting up like the neck of an old bottle and the slates holding the blue of the sky. It was autumn now and the drumlins would be pale with barley stubble and the countryside red with ferns and brambles and bucky briars and the last of the hedgerow fuschias; the air had the smokiness of burning coal and peat briquettes. He was homesick but felt he couldn't go home any more. He didn't think he was worthy of that cosiness now. He ran his parents the line that he worked for the Housing Executive.

Each morning he had to content himself with the sight of the giant corrugated palisade of the station, fortified like an ancient rath or ringfort. It gave him some comfort to see the walls spattered with paintbombs. He'd grown up within earshot of the army explosives range at Ballykinlar. The sound of mock battles carried in on the sea wind. It was no surprise he was mentally militarised and wanted the British out. Along Dundrum Main Street the Union Jacks were raised every July and would remain until shredded by the January gales. That was how he saw himself now. As a cold, unravelling wind that could dismantle the Protestant establishment.

Gerard slipped back behind his desk with another cup of coffee as John Rainey walked over.

'I've been watching you. You wee skiver,' accused Rainey, cock-a-hoop.

Uel, who was standing nearby, leapt to Gerard's defence.

'No, he isn't. You lay off him.'

'He's always skiving,' said John Rainey, prefacing his comments with a wink to Uel, trying to make it all seem a joke.

'But he isn't,' said Uel and Rainey laughed it off and cleared away.

'I suppose he was joking,' said Gerard, trying to defuse the situation, mindful that other staff were listening.

'A joke with a jag,' said Uel, lowering his voice. 'He's a jobsworth.

135

Can't stand him.'

Admittedly, Gerard had been taking every opportunity he could to get out of the office. He was bored by the form-filling, aware of the charade, and every morning he woke up racked with nerves wondering if this was the day that Sean was going to issue instructions.

He bumped into Uel again later at the canteen.

'I hope you don't think I'm never in my chair,' he said.

'Aye, well. Your mind is elsewhere. Bound to be. I suspect you have secret ambitions.' When Gerard looked flustered, Uel added, 'I mean, you've a degree and that there, haven't you?'

In the afternoon Gerard looked around the office and wondered if the blond girl, Aine, who'd let slip she was from Turf Lodge, was like him. She fired him a sympathetic grin. For a second, he didn't have a clue why she looked so knowing, then realised it was because he'd glazed over. He gave himself a shake. For God's sake if he carried on this way, he'd be in the skank. There was still a clatter of files to work through by five o'clock. The trouble was he couldn't conform, he'd never settle into the ranks of the clerical army. He had the uncomfortable thought that he'd joined the IRA because he didn't know what else to do in life.

A helicopter was whirring loudly overhead.

'It's a chinook,' he mentioned and a couple of the staff looked at him. It was clear they were surprised that unmilitarised civilians should be tuned into types of helicopter.

And John Rainey marched in, as the big bejaysus man, the voice on the front line, to disseminate the latest news that police in north Belfast had been called out to a hoax bomb and then ambushed by nationalist youths.

'If they hadn't managed to radio, they'd have been roadkill,' said John Rainey, the rage bubbling up.

. Amidst all the 'shocking' and 'terrible, so it is,' Gerard felt a stab of triumph. Then, he saw Uel passing the office door and put his head back down to his forms. He realised that the disquiet he often felt at work was similar to the time he spent on a French exchange with a family in Lyons. It arose from the inability to communicate freely, the need to always check each individual word before you said it.

When Uel found out that Gerard lived in his part of town, he insisted on giving him a lift into work every day. Gerard accepted, as it would have seemed suspicious not to, but sometimes he couldn't get over it, him sitting in a car with a peeler-man, approaching the red mag light of a checkpoint and being waved through with a cheery laugh.

'That's the church I go to,' said Uel one morning, tapping at the window on his side.

'You're a presbie, are you?'

'I'll tell you an interesting fact. All my ancestors were Roman Catholics.' He smiled. 'Every Protestant comes from Roman Catholic stock.'

'My father's a Protestant,' said Gerard.

He didn't mind telling Uel, if anything it would act as a smokescreen for his views, but in the past his father's religion had always been a source of shame. He'd kept it a secret at primary school where the other kids would talk about Prods as black devils. Fortunately it was easy to conceal as his father's name was O'Hara. On Sunday morning when his mother used to take the children to mass, they would pass the open bedroom door where great snores and fumes of alcohol were emanating, tumbling out with cold air, and it struck him that his father really was the devil.

A schoolmate had once told him that if your Dad was Catholic but your mother was Protestant, you could still get into the Orange Order due to some archaic law of 'being born of a Protestant womb'. He'd felt cast out. By some divine cruelty his parents had got their denominations the wrong way round, but at the same time he almost gloried in coming from a Catholic womb and a recurring image of his unborn self was as an alabaster baby Jesus standing in a Marian grotto.

He accepted that the reason he had joined the IRA could in part have been to get back at his father who often behaved, in his eyes, like a selfish bastard to his mother. 'Pack your bags then!' his father would shout at her if crossed. He'd speak of 'my house,' 'my chair,' exercising the same territorialism that had split the land in two.

It was inevitable that Uel would ask one night if he fancied a wee dot

137

around the pubs. Gerard made his excuses and went back to his bedsit. He switched the heat on. The place was fairly cosy but there was damp in the kitchen that split the paint on the pipes and twisted it into a type of coral. When he switched on the news, he saw activists picketing the Andytown barracks, calling for the NIPS to disband, and he half wished he was there with them, not inside a station but outside, kicking up a shindy. He'd heard the rumours, though, that Sinn Fein were about to join the Policing Board and it made him furious. Uncle Gerry would sell them out at the drop of a fiver. Adams couldn't deliver milk. The same men who conspired to kill Finucane were top detectives. You had to fight to show them you wouldn't take it.

He started to jiggle his leg with nerves. There were two staved-in bits in the cheaply made door. They looked like kick marks and he wondered who had lived here before.

He went into the bathroom for a shower and looked at himself in the mirror. He liked the mirror in here, it was broad, wide-screen instead of the narrow vertical ones he was used to. It brought in the whole bathroom, gave his face a broad backdrop, taking away from the examination of self in isolation.

The whiteness of the bathroom reminded him of the fresh-painted Laganside apartment where he'd gone to meet Sean.

'I've seen you educated kids before,' Sean said. 'Bellyless when it comes to the bit.'

Gerard managed to convince Sean of the power of his mind. He believed it himself. At university whenever he'd come home steaming from a night at the pub, he'd gone up to his room and opened a book and started to read, struggling against the dizziness. He hated not having control over himself.

'Can you make the ultimate sacrifice for your country?' Sean questioned.

'Yes,' nodded Gerard, his eyes gritty with fear. There. It was said. But in the back of his mind his idea of martyrdom from childhood had always been a shrapnel wound, the loss of a limb at most. It was 'hail the conquering hero in defeat,' coming back from rebellion with a pronounced limp, sustained in saving a fallen comrade in a dark field somewhere in

138

Mourne country. Death wasn't an option.

Gerard watched how Aine walked across the office, the impact of her heel on floor sending a quiver through her cheek with each step. Often she would sit nursing her chin in the cradle of her hand as she looked around the office, her curled fingers crumpling her nose. Or she would sit abstractedly strumming her upper lip with her finger, a gesture he found sexual. When he went back to his work, he could still hear her heavy silver bracelet clanking against the desk like a manacle.

John Rainey was holding forth about a documentary he'd seen on TV the night before.

'Crucifixion was a nasty business. Firstly, they drove the nails into the wrists, not the hands which is a common misconception.' He held up his hand to illustrate. 'See, there's only cartilage, so a nail would rip right through it. In actual fact the victims died by drowning.'

There were various groans of distaste and disbelief.

'See, they sank forward on the cross like this and their lungs filled with water,' he explained, ducking forward like a ski-jumper about to land. 'That's why the Romans had to break their legs to finish them off.'

'You sick bastard,' called Uel, grinning from the door.

'It's only history,' said John Rainey. 'It's interesting.'

'See your mind? It's the chamber of horrors. Even dark thoughts are afraid to go in,' said Uel and they all fell about laughing.

'No need to tear the arse out of it,' John Rainey grumbled but he hung around, wanting to bask in the attention.

That evening, feeling a sense of kinship in despising John Rainey, Gerard finally agreed to pop in with Uel to an East Belfast pub. He was nervous about going in. It was irrational but he couldn't help feeling as if he had something concealed on his person like a weapon or drugs that could fall out at any moment. Once inside, the crackle of conversation was like anywhere he'd ever known.

The lads at the bar greeted Uel warmly and gave welcoming nods to Gerard.

They both ordered Guinness and sat down at a table. Uel absent-mindedly painted a swastika with his finger in the Guinness head.

'What's that?' asked Gerard.

'Oh, just a protest against Irish fascism. It's instead of the shamrock.' He was embarrassed. 'Sorry. To be honest, I'm not that political.'

'Me neither.'

Gerard shifted uncomfortably under the shadow of his own lie.

Uel pointed out the blown-up photo on the wall behind them. The men who signed the Ulster Covenant stood in proud alignment but the face of a teenaged boy beamed out at the edge of the photo. No one, Uel said, had ever discovered the identity of that boy.

Gerard took a deep drink. Brown bubbles were drying on the side of his pint glass like stones in a boulder wall.

They talked about the office for a while.

'That Aine's a lovely girl,' said Uel.

'She is,' said Gerard, shyly looking into his pint.

'You'd better make a move before John Rainey asks her out. I mean, what girl wouldn't fall for his 'Ten Methods to Kill a Human Slowly'?"

'Method one – listen to John Rainey. Yesterday he was going on about all his trips to New York.'

'As if!' exploded Uel. 'Oh, he's been all over the States all right. Rathcoole, Deerpark...'

Gerard hadn't laughed so much in months as he did that night with Uel. His mother had always said to them as children, 'There'll be a shower in the mountains for all that laughing.'

He imagined his own mother's words of disavowal if things ever came to light.

'No, I don't know where he got it from. We never brought him up to hate. For God's sake, I even have the Princess Diana mugs on the mantelpiece.'

And his Dad would drink and drink the pain away. And he remembered the time his Dad had told him he was a spoilt bastard and should have been drowned at birth just because he'd forgotten to tape 'The Bill' one night. Or perhaps that was unfair. The outburst owed more to a long-standing anger at Gerard's thoughtlessness.

'Is it normal to have doubts?' he asked Sean a few days later.

140

Sean turned his keys over in his fingers and gave a tolerant nod. It was a Mercedes key-ring, Gerard observed, though there was nothing else about Sean to denote that he'd made good. He was a big Belfast man with blunt features and reddish hair, hoary at the tips and badly in need of a cut. He was wearing the same job-lot black t-shirt as on the first occasion they'd met.

'Yes. Believe you me, the worst are full of passionate intensity. I'm confident in you, Gerard. Our best soldiers always come from non-fanatic families. We want thinkers, not just doers.'

'It's easier to do something when you don't know the people involved.'

'Are you in love with an officer?' Sean's voice had suddenly turned sharp.

'Oh, no.'

Sean took a drag from his cigarette, twisting his mouth, almost chewing the smoke. His eyes were aquamarine in the sun splitting through the window.

'Well, then. Didn't you tell me you were prepared to make a sacrifice for your country, your people?'

'Yes, I said I would.'

'Would. You should never answer hypothetical questions with hypothetical answers.'

Gerard suddenly felt empty. He trawled inside himself desperately for the Republican doxology in which he'd trained himself for years but nothing came to mind. It had been so different in the first meeting with Sean when he'd quoted the words of Bobby Sands, 'Our revenge will be the laughter of our children,' like a schoolboy undergoing an oral exam, eager to impress.

He understood that Sean was asking him to do his 'duty.' But duty was a Protestant byword. Surely the nationalist anthem was justice.

'Remember, our struggle is about the community, not about the individual,' Sean impressed on him, raising his eyebrows, distorting the lines of his forehead.

There was something vulnerable and at the same time dangerously intelligent about the set of Sean's face. Gerard was gripped by the memory of a boy with that exact expression who had been bullied badly at

141

school. The same boy had become obsessed with military history and used to regale his classmates with tales about the heads of United Irishmen impaled on stakes.

'Perhaps you want to leave here,' said Sean, deliberating. 'Go to England for a while.'

Gerard wasn't sure what he meant, didn't want to know.

'No. I'll do it,' he assured Sean quickly.

People's umbrellas were moving along the streets like wibbling coloured jellies. The car ploughed up the fresh morning rain and through breaks in the hedge Gerard could see the cemetery stretching greenly. They slowed to a standstill opposite an old Celtic cross half-hidden behind the elderberries like the sights of a gun homing in on a target.

Uel fiddled with the reception on the radio.

'You look like a minister,' he chuckled, nodding at the way Gerard was sitting with his hands clasped together on his lap. 'Dearly beloved brethren... '

Gerard was turning it over in his head. Sean wanted the list of police names, addresses and registration numbers. Probably he would let them fall into the hands of the Continuity IRA or some other dissident strand which meant that Gerard's act was not to pull the trigger but to point the gun in the right direction. He knew from his own research that the boys who did the killing were handpicked to be less intelligent. The Shankill bomber who'd blown himself up in the chip shop with six civilians had only possessed an IQ of seventy. Many other freedom footsoldiers ended up in mental institutions. For the smarter ones it was clean hands and a dirty conscience.

He was exhausted. He hadn't slept for the thought that he could be condemning Uel to death. Betrayal had been the nightlong cry in his head and he was scared what Sean might do if he baled out. And he cursed this little country of collective rage and individual decency. And only at five a.m. had he fallen asleep after settling on a compromise. He would photocopy the file, delete Uel's name and try to take a fresh photocopy. He hoped to God he had the guts to take the risk.

John Rainey was walking down the corridor in close conversation with a senior officer as Gerard entered the building. Gerard panicked for a second that it was himself under discussion. He glanced back at them as they passed by, expecting them to sneak a tell-tale look at him, but they walked on oblivious.

Gerard took his seat and logged on.

The water dispenser gave a throaty gurgle, followed by a long, fathomless shudder. Some papers stuck to Gerard's hands like sticky tape.

He looked across to Aine's desk and saw that it was empty. All the papers had been cleared away. He felt his stomach sink. Without the girl with the Republican name he was alone, in cahoots with no one. It crossed his mind that Sean might have told her to go, in case it all went belly-up and she got implicated too. Christ sake, he kicked himself. He was being paranoid. She was just another pen-pusher. She was probably on a sickie and her papers had been farmed out to the other staff. No wonder everyone had their heads down.

'Is Aine away?' he asked his colleagues and they shrugged.

He thought it best to delay going to the filing cabinet till the afternoon by which time most of the staff would be bored and looking for any excuse to be up on their feet for a wander. The photocopier would also be freed up by then.

The morning passed and at lunch when he went to the canteen, Uel, who was sitting alone, beckoned him to come over. He looked serious and Gerard felt a dread.

'Don't tell the others yet,' Uel said quietly, 'but Aine's been arrested for spying.'

'Now why doesn't that shock me?' garbled Gerard. 'There was something watchful about her.' He couldn't believe his luck. 'And her name, Aine. From Turf Lodge. I'm surprised she even passed the security check.'

'It was a perfect cover. She was working for loyalist paramilitaries.' Uel sunk his head lower as other staff passed. 'She was some slick operator. She already got the information out to some safe houses all over Belfast before we tracked her. Gerard, we're going to inform the whole office that the file she copied wasn't police records. It contained the names and addresses of civilian staff.'

Gerard licked his dry lips.

'I don't want to scare you,' continued Uel, 'but inside the file was a copy of one photo. Yours. Special Branch will talk to you later about security measures.'

The shock was genuine. He was so used to dissembling   , he was stunned, disoriented. He watched Uel's hand reach comfortingly towards his shoulder.

He walked back to the office, feeling the cameras targeted on his head, feeling as if he was in some vast deadly game of pin the donkey. He sat down at his desk, trying not to betray any emotion. He rehearsed his words to Sean, 'I'm a target, you've got to pull me out of here, they know who I am, make me disappear,' and for a second he thrilled at the chance to escape.

The floor vibrated with heavy steps. In a glance he saw that John Rainey, accompanied by two men in plain clothes, had buttonholed one of his colleagues at the door.

A confusion came over him. And he could see across the corridor to how the rain stippled the puddles on the tarmac outside sending out great interlocking circles like a Celtic design. First widening, then tightening. Part of him wondered if this was the way the IRA bound you forever in conformity.

A large fly was zipping past his head in a shallow arc and he flicked it away with his hand. It alighted on his table, its head jerking like a faulty monitor. He rolled up a wad of papers, preparing for the kill.

The Second Coming of Teddy Lyons

Eoin O'Connor

"Did you hear Teddy Lyons is dead?" said Ger.

Sean stubbed out his cigarette and immediately started to roll another one. "Who? The name rings a bell."

"Teddy Lyons. From Silver Street. Brother of Ollie's," said Ger.

"Ollie with the hump?" said Sean.

"Now you have him. Here's a goal," said Ger.

They were in Dukes pub, gazing listlessly at Sky Sports' Monday night bottom of the table boreathon – Norwich vs Ipswich, fifty – nine minutes played, 0-0; "… a pulsating atmosphere here at Carrow Road as befits a keenly contested local derby," according to the commentator. Apart from Ger and Sean, the owner Matt Dillon, a solitary, brooding drunk at the bar and an elderly couple sitting speechlessly over soft drinks, the bar was empty. A pulsating atmosphere in Dukes of Nenagh.

"He should have scored that," said Ger.

Dukes was a John Wayne theme pub. The walls were decorated with photographs and movie posters featuring the actor in some of his best known roles, along with an assortment of memorabilia – stetsons, lassoes, chaps, a pair of spurred cowboy boots, an eye-patch, two green F.C.A berets and a World War One Prussian helmet that Matt Dillon maintained was very similar to the headgear Wayne had sported as Genghis Khan in *The Conqueror*. Displayed prominently behind the bar was Matt's pride and joy, a photograph of him shaking hands with the man himself. "Taken in Las Vegas in the Sands Hotel in 1973," as Matt

145

never tired of telling people. "Dying of cancer he was. But dying like a man!" And here he would usually turn away, overcome with emotion.

There were some among the pub's clientele who claimed that the closest Matt had ever been to Las Vegas was watching Buck Ryan's Sammy Davis Junior impersonation – performed annually, without fail at the Lion's Club Christmas party. What's more, Sonny Burke swore to God that he had seen that very same picture before, that it was actually Stewart Granger the Duke was shaking hands with and that all Matt had done was cut out Granger's head and substitute his own in its place. If one studied the photograph carefully, and many had, Matt's head did indeed seem to be balanced atop his body at an alarming angle and his neck seemed to have mysteriously vanished. However, any dark mutterings concerning the photograph's authenticity were kept strictly among the patrons. Matt could turn very peculiar when it came to John Wayne and all matters Wayne-related. He had famously barred Maurice Sullivan and his entire family because one night Maurice – always more of a Gary Cooper man – had had the temerity to refer to *The Shootist* as *The Shiteist*.

"And the man half dead when he making it!" Matt had fumed afterwards, before the inevitable turn away that always ensued when the subject of Wayne's demise came up.

Tonight Matt was ensconced at the end of the bar, radiating his customary sullenness, his huge back turned defiantly to the screen and the foreign game he detested. He had only turned it on because Ger had asked him to and only then with a great air of weary disgust. Sean and Ger never missed a match. Friday night Nationwide League, the occasional Saturday morning fixture, Ford Super Sunday, Monday Night Football, midweek Champions League, Scottish football, La Primera Liga, any match that was transmitted live would find them in Dukes, always at the same table directly in front of the big screen, always impassively observing irrespective of whether it was a drab fixture, like that night's, or a goal- and incident-packed thriller. Televised football was the centre of their lives. Both were unmarried and unemployed and likely to remain so, both were spectacularly uninterested in practically everything else life had to offer but when it came to televised football their devotion was absolute, going way beyond the boundaries of what was reasonable or sane or healthy. They would brave the most adverse weather conditions, shrug off debilitating illnesses, even ignore the funerals of acquaintances and family members in order to be in Dukes for a live match, any live match. Matt had no great affection either for them or for their woman's sport but he was glad of the business all the same. Times were tight.

Normally they spoke very little during a match, their comments being confined to the action, or the lack of it, on the screen or the citing of precedents (both, not surprisingly, had an encyclopaedic knowledge of the game). Tonight, however, was different. The death of Teddy Lyons was big news.

"When did he die? Last I heard he was in England," asked Sean.

"Died in England," said Ger. "Fell under a train. A tube. In bits, so he was. My mother was telling me. She was talking to Bridget Mac."

"A train," said Sean. "Did he jump or what?"

"Bridget Mac says he was drunk," said Ger. "She says he went off the rails completely over there. The daughter – you know, Anne – is living over there and she went to the Nenagh reunion and she met Teddy Lyons and she said he was like a wino. Out of his head, she said, and the arse hanging out of his trousers. On drugs as well she said."

"Jesus, he was some footballer. Didn't he have a trial when we were in school?" said Sean.

"Preston North End," said Ger. "Didn't get it though. Went to London then and went off the rails."

Sean shook his head ruefully and took an enormous mouthful from his pint. He was a small, boyish man whose age could have been anything from twenty to forty although his hair, which he wore down to his shoulders, was liberally streaked with grey and suggested he was closer to the latter than the former. He was dressed almost entirely in denim – denim jacket, denim shirt, denim jeans – and on his feet he wore a heavy scuffed pair of black boots. Ger was taller and heavier than Sean and appeared to be the older of the two as his hair had begun to succumb to male-pattern baldness (in fact, he was the younger by two years). He too wore the same black boots and denim jeans as Sean, along with a black leather biker jacket and a black T-shirt emblazoned with the word

147

'Triumph' and a logo consisting of a leering, Nazi-helmeted winged skull above a pair of crossed daggers. He also wore a gold sleeper in his left ear, which he attached as soon as he left his house and was careful to remove before he returned because his mother didn't like him, or indeed any person, male or female, wearing earrings. The pair's most striking feature, however, was their complete lack of expression. Regardless of the circumstances they remained, invariably, as frozen-faced as some repeatedly face-lifted old Hollywood actor. Nothing could faze them it seemed, not even the death of Teddy Lyons, which now appeared to have been exhausted as a topic of conversation.

Finally Sean broke the silence.

"Preston North End," he said and shook his head again.

Ger, without taking his eyes from the screen, said, "Would've been better off if he'd stayed here."

Sean looked around. The drunk at the bar had emerged from his stupor and was barking incoherently at Matt – something concerning drink being cheaper in England as far as Sean could tell – and Matt was nodding, employing the barman's art of appearing to be thoroughly absorbed in what he was hearing while actually being completely oblivious to it. Meanwhile the male half of the elderly couple was returning gingerly from the bar, walking with baby steps, as if it was nitro-glycerine and not Seven-Up in the glasses he was carrying. On the big screen the blue-and-yellow-shirted figures drifted about hopelessly, their reflections likewise on the front of a framed poster of *The Quiet Man*, John Wayne grabbing Maureen O'Hara with a crazed look in his eyes. And Teddy Lyons lay in a London morgue as Ger went up to the bar for more pints and Sean rolled another cigarette and a feeble shot from a Norwich player rolled harmlessly into the Ipswich goalkeeper's hands.

It could have been Teddy Lyons up there, thought Sean. Talk about a player. If anyone from here was going to make it …

He thought back to when he was about eight or nine and the matches on Knockanpierce Green that he'd played in nearly every day of the summer. You'd show up in the morning and there would always be someone there with a ball, one or two anyway, and there'd be a kick around, maybe a few games of three goals in while they waited for the

148

rest of them to come. When enough people had arrived, two teams were formed and the game would begin, a game that would continue for hours on end with people drifting away and returning, and others showing up and joining in during its course. There were few rules and almost zero strategy; whoever had the ball simply ran with it and everyone else followed so that the ball came to resemble a child magnet, dragging a trail of boys in its wake. This being an all-day affair, the scores achieved quickly became ludicrous − 84-79, 66-64, 80-76 and so on − and inevitably, almost every day, there would be a screaming match or a punch-up or both or several of each as to the exact state of the score. There were no referees in Knockanpierce back then, only mob rule and what the mob decreed was generally, if sometimes grudgingly, accepted. As haphazardly as the games commenced so too they concluded, petering out as the evening drew in and the light began to fail and the exhausted participants drifted away. The following morning, the whole ramshackle enterprise would creak into life again and so it went for the duration of the summer months.

Sean had played every day and although he had a certain doggedness that stood to him in the bear pit of the Green, he had no real aptitude for the game. The ball refused to do anything he wanted it to while his feet, when presented with a ball, would lapse into cluelessness and he could only look on in frustration as his attempted through balls and shots on goal ballooned away in bizarre directions. All his hours of practice, all the skill tips he studied in his weekly copy of *Shoot*, all his close scrutiny of Kenny Dalglish and his attempts at mimicking him, it was all to no avail. You either had talent or you didn't and Sean learned early on, to his immense (and continuing) disappointment, that when it came to soccer he was to be doomed to mediocrity. Nevertheless, with the single-mindedness of the obsessive he persevered, in spite of his lack of natural ability. He showed up religiously at the Green every day and played, possessed by the belief that eventually, given enough practice and work and experience, he would achieve the status in the eyes of others that the likes of Teddy Lyons held in his. He would become one of the elite, the little gods of the Green, the select band of adepts who seemingly had the world, in the guise of an orange plastic football, at their feet.

Teddy Lyons. He was about twelve at the time and to the nine-year old Sean, he was a god. Not that he looked like a god or anything, in fact far from it. With his skeletal frame, bright red hair and freckle-spattered face, he resembled a Swan Vesta match come to life. He walked with a peculiar bandy-legged gait as if he spent his life on horseback and his face wore a permanent smirk, something that infuriated teachers and parents and most adults, for some reason. They were forever telling him to wipe it off of his face, calling him a young pup, telling him they'd soften his cough for him. To them he was a brazen, smart-arsed little fecker who'd want to cop himself on and the thing is, they were right. He was everything they said he was. Doubtless there were other factors responsible for his being so but to Sean and the other players on the Green, the explanation was simple. Teddy Lyons was a footballing genius and out of this arose his insolence and apparent contempt for school and authority and rules and all the rest of the crap that the adult world held so dear. Because Teddy Lyons didn't need any of it. Not where he was going. And Teddy Lyons was going places, that was a certainty, and anyone who saw him on the Green couldn't but agree.

How could he not be? Look at him, receiving an awkward thigh-level pass and killing it stone dead, effortlessly, before setting off on one of his lazy strolls with the ball, loping along dopily until someone dares attempt to challenge him, some clown like Sean charging towards him, and Teddy seems to pause for an instant, as if pondering the foolish pretensions of these novices and why they even bother, the ball held lightly and tantalisingly beneath his left foot, waiting until his challenger is within inches of him before, with the rapidity of a rubber band snapping, he drags the ball back, out of the range of the oncoming clodhopper feet and with an impossible, mesmerising shimmer of feet and a nonchalant body swerve he's gone, all of his earlier indolence evaporated as he sprints towards goal. Team-mates scream, "Teddy! Here!" and wave their arms in the air and any coach would tell him that here, right now, he should look up, look for a team-mate, release the ball; there's three opposition players coming for him for Jesus' sake, release it, release it and continue your run. Teddy can see his team-mates all right, he can hear them shouting, "Teddy! Here! Teddy!", he can see the three opponents (a smudge of puff

150

and bluster) bearing down on him and the tamed ball doing his foot's bidding and in the distance, the two caged trees that served as goalposts getting ever closer. He's conscious of everything that's going on but you wouldn't think it to look at him. Jesus, he makes it look so easy, as if it's the most natural thing in the world! Look at the skinny little prick, there's three on him but look how he turns and guards the ball, makes a mockery of his assailants' attempts to dispossess him, those three sweaty, awkward yokels flailing away with idiot legs, and then he spins, slips the ball ahead of him and bursts through the by now totally bewildered clump of bodies around him, bouncing off one, then another and he's through! He's lost the ball for an instant but his leg stretches out, gathers it in and he's away again, leaving two yokels flat on their arses, one in vain pursuit, nothing but fresh air between him and the goal now. Dumbo Shanahan, who somehow always ended up playing in goal, comes squirming out of his area like a sack of drowning puppies, the very picture of a lack of co-ordination and now it's only a question of how Teddy will finish it. Will he let fly? Will he take it around Shanahan? Will he have a bit of crack, let Shanahan take the ball from him before contemptuously snatching it back, or has he some new trick to unveil? Not today. A simple chip wraps it up, Dumbo Shanahan's upstretched arms clawing thin air, the ball just out of reach, coming down almost directly in the centre of the imaginary goal line and trickling harmlessly to a halt. Someone shouts, "That's 18-12" and Teddy is strolling back to the opposite end of the green, smirk affixed to his face but otherwise casual as if he'd done nothing special, while Sean and the others looked on in awe and envy.

Every day of the summer Teddy Lyons had performed similar miracles on Knockanpierce Green. Later he had almost single-handedly propelled Nenagh Celtic's under-fourteen team to their most successful season ever. (Sean could still remember the grainy black-and-white photo on the sports page of the local paper – two rows of sniggering lads in outsize jerseys and baggy shorts behind a wall of trophies and Teddy among them, kneeling in the middle of the front row, tongue stuck out of the side of his mouth à la Benny Hill.) The general consensus among the town's soccer people was that young Lyons was some ball player, that he was feckin gifted, that he'd want to start thinking about a trial in England

and that he'd have no problem getting it if only he'd cop himself on and stop acting the bollix. Sean, at that time a member of the under-twelve side (included more for his diligence in attending training sessions than his ability, which hadn't significantly improved) had heard the stories and, like everyone else was shocked and secretly thrilled. Teddy Lyons, showing up three quarters of an hour late for training – *with a fag in his hand!* – and refusing to take part in laps of the pitch, saying he was a soccer player, not a racehorse. Teddy Lyons, calling Rody Ryan, the under-fourteen's coach, a baldy-headed fucker to his face. Teddy Lyons, after being sent off for a homicidal challenge during a cup match against Thurles, proceeding to attack the referee with a corner flagpole. Teddy Lyons involved in one outrage after another and always getting away with it, always coming out on the other side still smirking and none the wiser. He was regularly the recipient of dire warnings from the likes of Rody Ryan but they were wasting their breath. Anyway, what did they know? Teddy, like all geniuses, had nothing but contempt for those whom he regarded as hindrances to the realisation of his vision. If they'd had their way he would have been one of those sheep who *toed the line* and *respected an opponent*, a *good* lad, a *reliable* lad, *a team player*. Bullshit, all of it. Who had scored four goals in the second half against the Silvermines and they three-nil down at half time? Who had not only played the whole of the cup semi-final against Holycross with a broken collarbone but also scored a hat trick? Who, when they were down to seven men in that legendary bloodbath against Birdhill, had effectively taken on the entire opposing team on his own and scored the game's only goal in injury time? Some *team player*, was it? I'll tell you who it was, it was Teddy Lyons, Teddy Lyons from Silver Street, Daglish and Cruyff all rolled into one, the greatest soccer player Nenagh had ever seen, the one among them who was going to make it to all those places the rest of them could only fantasize about. It was unspoken of course – this was Nenagh, after all, and you wouldn't have lasted very long spouting that kind of old shite – but it was implicit in everything he did, everything he was and no-one doubted him, not for a second. Teddy Lyons was going to make it. It was only a matter of time.

And now he was dead. Well, thought Sean, people die. His own father had died a few years ago and his mother not long afterwards. Others he had known, lads and girls, had died too, everything from car crashes to drowning to house fires to suicide. People die and that's it, there's nothing you can do about it. Go to the funeral, shake hands, watch the box descending into the hole, get drunk afterwards. Two weeks up the road and it's as if they'd never existed. Sean was singularly untroubled by the deaths of others and it wasn't strictly true to say he was shocked or upset by the death of Teddy Lyons because essentially, he wasn't. Yet something was bothering him. While Ger continued to stare at the screen, Sean had lost all interest in the East Anglia derby and was staring into the depths of his pint, that one phrase of Ger's repeating in his head: "Would've have been better off if he'd stayed here." If he had stayed, Sean thought, he'd be sitting somewhere right now, watching this game. Maybe even here in Dukes. Older now, heavier than he used to be, years of weekend porter having thickened up his midriff. His oul lad probably would have got him a job in the glass factory where he had worked since the mines closed down. He'd be married too, with a couple of kids and a house in Conlon's Road. Quieter now. Mature. An adult. Gave up soccer a long time ago, still had a kick around with his son in the back garden now and then but otherwise he's too wrecked of an evening, and too unfit. Promises himself every new year that he's going to take it up again, get back into shape, maybe organise a five-a-side league with the lads at work but has forgotten about it before January is out. Still follows the game though. Sunday afternoons, Monday nights, Wednesday nights, the occasional Saturday morning fixture, there's Teddy in the pub, squeezed into a Liverpool jersey, gaze fixed on the big screen, slowly hoisting a pint of porter to his mouth. Could there be any doubt about it? Of course he'd have been better off if he'd stayed. Preston North End! Fairytales, thought Sean, as if life was a book or a film or something. He should have copped himself on and not gone off making an eejit out of himself. Look where it got him. Look where he ends up! A piss-soaked wino, weaving along the edge of a station platform with a train coming towards him. Scraped off the track and in bits in a black bag in a London morgue. How low can you sink? And to think I used to look up to him! It'd make you laugh. Some genius. Some destiny.

153

Ger heaved himself out of his chair with some difficulty and said, "Can't see much happening in this now. A load of bollix. Going for a piss."

Sean looked at the screen. Still 0-0, into the last few minutes, both sides now reduced to hefting long, aimless balls into each other's penalty areas.

"It's quite literally going to take a little something extra special to inject a spark of life into this, so to speak," said the commentator.

The sooner this was over the better, Sean decided. He dumped the change from his pockets onto the table and began to count it to see if he had enough for another round. Stay and watch You're On Sky Sports after this, he was thinking. Go home, catch The Premiership on ITV at half eleven. I hate this new money. Then he looked up at the screen and froze.

The camera was on a player in the yellow of Norwich jumping up and down on the touchline behind the referee's assistant.

"Bit of a last ditch throw of the dice this by Norwich, preparing to introduce the young Irishman," said the commentator.

The referee's assistant held up the electronic board and the camera switched to a frazzled-looking Norwich player who, having seen his number held aloft, began to jog towards the touchline.

"A lot of buzz around this young man, let's see if he can turn the tide in Norwich's favour in the dying stages," said the commentator.

Substitute and substituted high-fived and the former sprinted onto the pitch as the announcement boomed out of the Carrow Road P.A: "Substitution for Norwich, number seven Darius Bracknell replaced by number sixteen, Teddy Lyons."

Sean stood up, pointed, sat back down. He looked around to see if anyone else had realized what had just happened but the bar was now deserted except for Matt and his drunken friend, crouched in a conspiratorial huddle, deep in conversation.

It can't be, thought Sean. I'm cracking up.

Yet when he looked up at the screen again there he was, Teddy Lyons, trotting backwards over the halfway line as the Norwich keeper prepared to take a goal kick. Teddy Lyons! Somehow or other he hadn't changed – he looked exactly the same as he had the last time Sean had seen him immediately before he'd left for England, still a skinny little ginger prick.

This is crazy, thought Sean, it can't be … but it is. It is. It's him.

"It is him," he said aloud. "It's fuckin Teddy Lyons!"

The match was into injury time by now.

"A loose pass from Herriot, possession again squandered by Ipswich," said the commentator. "Picked up by Lyons."

As Sean watched, Carrow Road disappeared, the pitch and the stands melting away, metamorphosing into a patch of green in the middle of a crescent of houses upon which a gang of boys ran in pursuit of an orange plastic ball. It was late in the evening and there were only a handful of players left now. A few of the erstwhile participants, among them Sean, had stayed to observe the dregs of the day's play and were sprawled on the dampening grass on the side of the Green and behind the goal. A precious cigarette was passed around and argued over while on the field of play it was decided that the next goal would be the winner.

"A terrific burst of pace from Lyons," said the commentator, his voice going up an octave.

"There's Lyons off," someone said. Sean could just about make him out, a slender silhouette in the thickening gloom streaking through a series of tired challenges, and as he watched him charge inexorably towards his destination, he felt the familiar sensations arising; a cocktail of admiration, self-pity, jealousy and begrudgery, all jostling for supremacy within him. Tonight, though, he sensed a new addition to the ensemble and wasn't quite sure why. After all, what was there to be sad about?

"Can he go all the way here?" shrieked the commentator.

Of course he can! He's Teddy Lyons, Teddy Lyons from Silver Street, and he's going to take on the world.

He's past the last player, he takes the ball around the prone form of the goalkeeper, draws his foot back …

… and sends the ball wide of the right-hand post.

"You fuckin eejit you," someone shouts.

"Oh my word, with the goal gaping at his mercy, how on earth did he contrive to miss that?" wailed the commentator.

Ger came back from the toilets just as the full time whistle was blown.

"What happened?" he asked.

Sean was silent as he rolled and lit a cigarette. When he looked up, Ger was amazed to see that his eyes were filled with tears.

Grace

Lara Fergus

God is still here, in the small spaces between the houses. In the thoughts of some, in different ways. In the rules for everyone. So is sin. For girls Maeve's age, sin sucks God from your body and takes nine months to do it. Every woman in this village knows that.

Maeve can see it in the curl of their shoulders. The way they hook their handbags in the crook of their arms and pull them tight over their stomachs. Sees the suspicion in Mrs Gerahty's red eyes, the life-raft grip in her knuckles as she drives her shopping trolley past. The desperation in Mrs Simpson's arms, punching in the deep-freeze. All that grasping. They must have had plans, once, thinks Maeve. Had God in their young veins, pumped pink with hope. Now they all look the same. God leached out. A slow murder, unremarked.

'Will he know the difference d'you think, dear?' asks Mrs Simpson, a frozen pie at arm's length to read the small print.

'Sorry?' says Maeve.

'Never mind.' Gestures with the pie packet. 'Your Ma wants you.' She gives Maeve a limp smile before joining Mrs Gerahty at the bakery counter. Maeve looks down the aisle to where her Ma flags three baby jumpsuits.

'Which one, love?'

Maeve moves slow as an ice-breaker, her eight-month belly carving a path. She thinks, it doesn't matter. There are no more choices. I'm already Mrs Gerahty, Mrs Simpson, my Ma.

'They all look the same,' she says.

Her Ma drops one into the trolley. Pink for girls. The women on the way back from the bakery pass with a hello to her Ma. Maeve knows they'll wait until the next aisle before whispering. They are not cruel, like the kids at school, they understand. This is the definition of compassion, Maeve remembers from her Sunday school classes, to *suffer with* somebody. It suffocates her, this communal suffering. She has never wanted to live in their world, and their sympathy insists that she does. She grips the side of her Ma's trolley.

'Don't feel sorry for me,' she says after them. Loud enough to hear, though they pretend they don't.

'Maeve!' says her Ma, 'Don't go making such a fool of yourself.'

Maeve looks at the thin bars of the trolley between her fingers and wants to hit her head against them, to draw blood.

Her faith had been sea-deep. Rare for a girl her age, almost incompatible. God poured through her body like water through sand. As a child her happiest place was the cold of the church, her hair plaited at the nape of her neck, her clean hands in her lap. Everyone breathing mist except the priest. He breathed the Word and was warm with it. He wove a blanket of words to warm them through winter. God was in the warp and the weft. He cast a close-woven net upon them and touched them with words. I am a fisher of men, he said. Maeve listened for God. The priest took a breath. God was in the silences. He filled the arched body of the church. She grew in that place. Her body formed its curves, and God pumped through the veins of her sinful flesh. Jesus was all-forgiving. Maeve was glad to hear it.

Checkout. Catherine O'Malley working it, sliding the tins through the laser beam, mild as the Magdalene. Maeve knows that it was never the 'flu keeping her from school that time. All the women know. They said it was adding murder to your sins, but my God, look at the result. Purged of her sin, her pink-tinted face flushed with relief. She was earning money, going to uni in September. Science. She had a choice and she chose life. Catherine smiles when she sees Maeve, leans over the counter and touches her belly. 'Must be nearly cooked,' she laughs. Maeve feels sick. Feels resentment kicking her from inside. Would murder to change places. Wants the pink tint, wants to find smiling again. Catherine spins to check a price with her colleague. Look at her, how lightly she moves.

Even when she reached That Age, nobody had thought Maeve would be one. Nobody had thought of her at all, with that quiet face, buttoned collar. It had annoyed her, those assumptions. That if you didn't screech and laugh it must be because you had nothing to screech and laugh about. At school she ate her lunch alone. She got good marks, though. She wasn't dumb, despite what they said now.

Not surprising, though, that her sin was silence. She'd never said much and now she hadn't said no. Three times, in fact, but all with the same boy and she had liked him at first. He had thick black eyebrows and was a silent type himself. And it felt strong to be there, her, Maeve, doing it like the other girls, the ones who smirked in class like they knew something different, something better. Felt womanly, at first, the boy smiling at her, locking the car doors.

'You're not just teasing, I hope?'

And she wasn't, she smiled back, even when she felt small as a child again, him too big, the doorhandle pushing into her back. Praying for the pain to stop. She kept silent. For two more Saturdays. So that he was her boyfriend, and she wasn't a slut.

By that time the school knew. What was expected in other girls was grotesque in Maeve Baxter. The church-goer, the book-reader. She'd applied for theology at uni, for Christ's sake. It was laughable. She had no-one to tell when her period didn't come. She turned the boy away and shut herself up in her room after school. Waited for the night, took a razor blade. Said five Hail Marys and four Our Fathers. She could not kill. But could not let live. She accepted small cuts, to her breasts and stomach, for relief.

She'd told the boy the next day. Waited till after school, took him by his coat sleeve to the park out the back. He said nothing, pulled his sleeve from her hand. Bent down, picked up a rock, rubbed at the dirt with it. She said 'Have you any money?' She was freezing, pulled her hat over her ears. 'I want to go over to Britain, to Holyhead.' She couldn't say the word. Neither could he.

'Be cheaper to do it here,' he said. Stood up, threw the rock at a tree.

She'd thought of that. Had nightmares of secrecy, car rides in the dark. Pain and blood. Being held down. 'On someone's kitchen table? Would you?' she asked, her voice high.

'Look, I can get you a phone number.'

She was terrified, furious, pushed him, her two hands, thump, against his chest. He stumbled backwards, regained balance. Breathed.

'It's safe,' he said, 'Catriona did it. She's fine.' His sister. Manages a hotel in Dublin. She's fine.

But there's the stories. The injuries, the deaths and the girls who just go missing.

The devil is in the details. In words said or not said, a few pounds here or there. Her mother hauls the plastic bags into the car boot and Maeve thinks maybe, if the boy had given her the money, she could have made it. Come back cleansed, be planning another life, her own, buying books instead of baby clothes. Imagine having choices again. It's a sin to still think of that, she's been told. Especially the way she does, with regret. You shouldn't regret a failed murder.

But it was fifty pounds just for the ferry, and she didn't even have that. 'Well, you won't get very far I'm afraid, love,' said the man behind the glass. Maeve had been awake all night on the bus to Dublin, sitting behind the driver, scarf up to her chin. The terminal was over-heated, her face flushed and she felt nauseous. The words scrambled at her, scratched, she rubbed her eyes with her palms.

She pushed herself from the counter. The floor pitched as she ran toward the loo. She suddenly needed to urinate, slammed the door, fumbled the lock and nearly missed the seat. The cubicle rocked around her and she sat there thinking Jesus. Jesus, save me.

Silence.

She was plumped with it. It stretched her breasts and her stomach. It was rooted into her and sucking, sucking God from her flesh. She had to get it out now, while she still had six months to go, six months' grace which God would let her keep if she could just be washed clean. She hit her head against the cubicle wall, then again, harder, so she screamed.

160

She could hear voices outside but screamed anyway. If she had a razor, take this, this is my blood, she would say, and wait for the seep. She needed something with her fists, some violence, hit at her head, her chest, the door. Thumping from both sides, and shouting now. 'This is my body,' she screamed, and clasped her hands to stop them flailing. Lord Jesus, think on me and purge away my sin. Stretched her arms out in front, breathed in. Punched her hands into her stomach with all her force. And again, in silence. And again.

The policeman pulled himself in under the door. Maeve watched him, didn't kick, but kept punching, faster. He grabbed her hands, said words in a quiet voice, words that fell around Maeve, making no sense, but calming, like snow. She stopped punching. In the car she looked at the back of his head, the bald patch shining in the passing headlights. She leaned forward to the holes in the perspex separating them. 'Can you help me?' she whispered. The man moved her eyes but didn't answer. 'You can't stop me going over,' she said, 'I read it in the paper. I just need money, fifty pounds. Please.' They stopped at the lights.

'I'm sorry love. You're too young.'

The news hit the house in a wave of shock and her Da looked drowned in his chair. Maeve thought, he should have let me tell them at least. She sat on the sofa with the policeman beside her. Her Ma was sitting forward with her hand on the teapot as if she had forgotten what to do next. The policeman said 'I won't take sugar, thanks.' Her Ma looked at him.

Later, Maeve took her Ma's sleeve. 'Please. Help me.'

But her Da was in the doorway.

'Don't look at me like that,' she said to him, 'It's less of a sin than having it, isn't it?' To her Ma 'Isn't it?'

Her Ma said, 'We haven't the money in any case.'

She sat cross-legged on her bed pressing her rosary to her forehead. Number fifty: Hail Mary, full of grace. She bit hard on the heel of her hand, there, holding the word 'grace' in her mouth, waiting for the sweet taste. The release of redemption. The word dried in her mouth. How could it be forgotten, a sin which would grow teeth and nails, walk, run, follow her, chase her, screaming? There were no words for the prayer she wanted.

God evaporated in the details. Silence was infecting the house.

The day after, Maeve stood behind the kitchen door and listened. Her Ma was gutting the chicken on the table behind her. From the living-room came voices and Maeve couldn't believe her ears.

'He'll marry her alright.'

It was the boy's father, a meatloaf man sitting with his hands on his thighs. The boy sat next to him picking at a loose thread on the sofa arm.

'It's the right thing to do. I told him that as soon as I knew about it myself.' He smiled at Maeve's Da, happy to be doing the right thing. Her Da smiled back and offered him a whiskey. The boy didn't look up.

Maeve laughed, turned to her Ma. 'They're joking.'

Her Ma turned away to wash her hands. Maeve would not stop smiling, would not let it be a straight-faced thing, laughed again and said 'For God's sake.'

Her Ma wouldn't laugh and wouldn't say anything either. Maeve went into the back garden and put her hands against the high stone wall. It's not the middle ages, she thought. It's my choice and I've two now. She went to the open kitchen window and said to her Ma 'I won't.' When she came inside her Ma said 'It would make everything easier, that's all,' and wiped the table.

Two weeks later it was Maeve's last-chance day and she was a long way from Holyhead. There was no stopping it now. She would be fat with sin. It would come out of her but never leave her. God would know. She stared at the curl of the holy water gripping her two fingers and thought 'meniscus,' a word from her physics class. An innocent word, so far away. She'd always liked the logic of physics, the perfection of God's universe. 'Come on, love,' said Mrs Simpson, standing behind her in her good cardigan, 'You can't absorb it, you know.'

The priest cast his net and God was there. The warp. The weft. The pattern and the knots. Maeve watched it floating down. Saw an emptiness above her, falling. The congregation breathed in. The air was sucked away. Maeve choked in the absence, could feel nothing. The priest spoke the Word. It swam everywhere but fished from her grasp, slippery as a newborn. She sank in her seat, weeping. God was gone. She was left holding nothing. She held out her hands.

Her elders showed the way. The path back to God was up the aisle. She was forgiven in a promise of love. Honour. Obedience. God narrowed to a single path that slithered from her sight. She signed the registry book. A child conceived guilty would be born innocent. Maeve was neither one nor the other. She was wife and would be mother. Approval felt like redemption. Everyone was smiling, and Maeve smiled back. Her mother cried.

Maeve went back to school. The staff found it inappropriate, more than one teacher said so. But her mother insisted, it could be useful, and there were just a few months before final exams. Maeve prefered it to sitting at home, waiting for the boy's graduation. But the more she showed the more of a freak she became. The other students avoided her, they didn't even laugh anymore. She didn't study, and when the university admission forms came round she threw hers out. There were the childbirth classes Thursday evenings. She was the youngest, and the others smiled at her politely.

On the way home from the supermarket she holds the seatbelt out from her belly, her face dark like a mask. It's summer, she's finished school and it's time to bury herself. Her old self, she means, the one who sleeps alone. Tomorrow's the honeymoon. Dublin. A discounted week in her sister-in-law's hotel. Then a job for the boy, a baby for her, a flat for the three of them. At the traffic lights one of her teachers crosses the road in front of the car. His face almost smiles at recognising a student, but then stops when it registers which one. Maeve realises that he, that all of them had just been waiting for it to finish. For her to be another supermarket wife instead of a pregnant schoolgirl. So that they could forget her.

On her narrow child bed she turns her rosary in her fingers. A thought is creeping through her. To forget is not to forgive. She has been betrayed, and in a church. A marionette marriage. Outside the house, the village prepares for bed. They will never forgive her. God is gone from her and she from God. She looks at the rosary. Just beads. A sadness comes into her bones. It seeps into her flesh, discolours it, stretches her skin. She puts down the beads and takes up her razor. She cuts in the soft places, to ease the pressure.

163

The next morning the boy stands beside her in the doorway of the honeymoon suite. They look at the queen-size bed with a floral print the same as the curtains. He goes in without a word, sits on the bed and flicks on the TV.

Maeve waits on the threshold. Then picks up her suitcase. 'I'm going for a walk,' she says. The boy doesn't look up.

It starts to rain as she walks to the jewellers. She gets a hundred pounds for the ring, much less than she expected, but enough, with what her Ma gave her as well. It's pouring when she leaves and she's soaked to her tight-pulled skin.

The ferry terminal is hotter than before and smells of sweat. There is thunder in the distance and the rain pelts the windows. She slips in her wet dress on the plastic chair and can't get comfortable. Only a half-hour wait, and not many people, it's the middle of the week. Then she feels it. A tightening inside her. Which tightens further, she draws in air, it peaks, washes away. She looks around. Did she groan, cry out? No, someone would have looked up. She has to stay quiet. They're false anyway, those pains, she thinks. But ten minutes later it comes again. She breathes in gulps, grips the sides of the chair until she's released. This is too soon. She has three weeks to go. She readies herself for the next one, though, just in case. When it comes she breathes as she was taught, but quietly. She has to get away.

On the ferry she finds the Ladies and no-one else is there yet, so she chooses the big one for wheelchairs and takes a towel from her suitcase to make a seat on the floor. Just a couple of hours, she thinks, and then a British hospital with no talk of husbands. She just needs to be alone, do the breathing.

They are out of the harbour now and thumped by the waves. There is a smell of rot and disinfectant. The wall curves against her back, metal-cool. She feels nauseous and the contractions are out of beat, twisting and not untwisting before twisting again. She kneels to vomit into the toilet bowl and a wave rocks her, her hand slaps against the door and she steadies but there's the pain again, wrenching and she's on her hands and knees saying 'help.' It was a mistake to come here, to be alone, she thinks, something's wrong.

'Help,' she shouts. Nobody comes. The boat's almost empty. She has to get to where there are people, stands up, sways. Again the clenching, mounting and her legs fold. She grips the hook on the back of the door and is washed with pain, all her body, her hand slips, grabs the hand basin, she has to lie down, bangs her hip as she falls, she thinks, is she breathing? Yes, she can hear it, fast, and there's a need in her body, a deep pressure, a need to push.

You're not allowed to. She remembers that. Not yet, you have to wait, something about dilation. She can't remember what dilation is, or when it happens. When can she push? It comes again, she does the breathing, the pain's gone but the pressure's incredible. She thinks, Jesus, it'll come before we reach Holyhead. She thinks, what'll I do? Then she thinks a different thought.

Someone comes into the room. Maeve sits down on the toilet. She hears the door of the cubicle next to her close, lock. The pressure comes again, intensifies, she tries to hold the sound inside her but can't, a groan escapes.

'Alright in there, dear?' An English woman. Middle-aged.

'Yes,' Maeve replies.

'Bit seasick, are you?'

'Yeah.'

She hears the flush and the woman washing her hands, leaving. Maeve says nothing. The thunder is getting louder and the waves slap the boat. With the next contraction she has to push, dilation or not, grabbing the toilet seat with both hands, her whole body bearing down. She thinks, they lie down in hospitals, so she lowers herself onto the wet floor. She bunches up her dress and pulls off her underpants. For waves and waves she pushes, feels the pressure on the bones, muscled nameless parts of her body, forces it to come, come quickly now. Jesus, it'll cry, she thinks, suddenly. People will come, she has to be quick, be prepared.

She finds her hands flat on the floor, up to her knees with the sea jolting her she grips the toilet seat and there are her feet and there's the windowsill now under her hands and she's hauled to standing and sees the dark surface of the sea, pocked with rain. Her hands grope for the heaviest thing, find the porcelain cover of the cistern, she needs both hands, pulls it to her chest, then hurls it at the window. It rebounds, bangs to the floor. The glass slivers into a web of cracks, but doesn't break. Maeve falls back into the door and stares, thinks, Jesus, goes to pick up the cistern cover and is clutched by another contraction, grabs the hand basin and stifles a scream as she feels it, a coil untwisting, a weight splitting through her.

She sways. Collects the folds of her dress and looks down. Puts her hand on the small, shocking head. Crumples to the floor. The boat lurches, flinging sweat from her face and there's no pressure anymore, just the so-small, too-big body unravelling out, shoulders coming torso arms slithering legs and feet.

She looks at it. Red as a devil. Silent as God. A wrinkled thing, with a head like a cone. Which starts to scream. Kicks. Urinates. Jesus, a little girl. Screaming air and spit. Maeve puts her hand over its mouth. Looks at it for a long time. Thinks God almighty as the placenta pushes out and lays on the feet of the baby, who kicks it off. She thinks, I can't play mother. Don't know how to. Wants to say sorry, but stops herself. Don't talk to it. She looks up at the cracked window.

She puts her hands on the toilet rim and pushes to her feet. She feels soft as sand. The cistern cover is loose in her grasp. She hauls it to her shoulder. And throws. The window shards in an explosion of sound. The glass flies over the sea and the porcelain rectangle angles from view. Maeve feels the blood pumping in her hands. She reaches down and picks up the baby, the gorged bag hanging from it by a blue cord. She stretches it out between the teeth of broken glass. Her arms are water. Her hands won't grip. There are no more choices. The baby slithers, slips, is caught briefly between fingers and palm, by the foot, is too heavy, falls.

She presses her forehead to the windowsill, feels the rain on her arms. Hears nothing, no splash, the storm is too loud, the waves too violent. She's rocked. Blood leaks from her arm, cut by the broken glass. She slides to the floor.

She feels nothing. The pain is a long way away. From where she sits she pulls at the toilet paper roll and starts mopping up the blood that rolls over the tiles with the waves. Her mind is white. She stops all thoughts, knows she can't think them. Not now. The cleaning takes a long time.

Standing, she holds the windowsill for balance and throws her dress and the towel into the sea. Takes clean clothes from her bag. She will believe it never happened. She says this to herself as she washes her legs and hands.

When she leaves the ferry at Holyhead, the tiredness hangs from her bones. After such a crossing, her pallor goes unremarked. Her skin feels raw under her dry clothes. She walks with unusual grace.

Andrew Lloyd-Jones

So there was this bloke on the bus the other day, and he was writing
down all this stuff, and me and Sarah were all like, what are you
writing, and he said he was writing this story or something. And we
said, so are you a writer then, and he said, I've written a few things,
and he said he'd like won the Canongate Prize and been in the Bridport
Prize collection or whatever. And then he said he was in advertising,
and he started talking about how he was writing a novel now, and
Sarah looked all serious and said, I think that's really interesting, and
then we both pissed ourselves because he thought we actually cared.
How sad is that? I think he said his name was like, Andrew or
something?

Geona Edwards

was born 6 July 1974. He grew up in Virginia.
He did an M.Phil in Creative Writing at Trinity, 1998-99.
Now living in Spain since Spring 2001, teaching English and Spanish,
writing short stories and poetry (haiku). He has just bought a big,
century-old house!

Katy Darby

is 26 and has been writing part-time since 1998. After her English
degree at Oxford she set the world of IT marketing ablaze before
realising that flogging servers for a living was rubbish. The result has
been thirty-odd short stories, a collection of poetry, 10 novels, four
plays and three screenplays, most of which are unpublished. There is
literally nothing the girl isn't foolish enough to try. She has also won
prizes for her poetry, plays and short stories, including the Frogmore
Prize for Poetry, and has twice been shortlisted for an Eric Gregory
Award. Please give generously.

Mia Gallagher

has been writing since she was eight. Early fiction was published in DCU college mag "Authaus", the University of Ulster Press and the *Sunday Tribune*, where her story "Departure" was nominated for a New Irish Writing award. Her story "Found Wanting" was published in last year's Fish Anthology. In 2001, her monologue "Normality" won Arts Council funding for development into a full-length play "The Mercy Visit". Mia has recently been commissioned to write a site-specific monologue for Galloglass Theatre Company.

Jason Bellipanni

lives and writes in New Hampshire. His highly entertaining, brilliantly revised, and as yet unpublished, *From a Pond of Slippery Devils: Stories*, received the 1999 Harcourt Brace Jovanovich Award for the best manuscript from the University of Colorado. He received a writing fellowship to the Vermont Studio Center in July 2001. He is working on a novel, a children's story about a giant's mouth, a screenplay about dishwashers, and a collection of essays centered on his relationship with the country of Italy. His work has won awards from *Writers' Digest* and has appeared in *The Cream City Review, The Berkeley Fiction Review*, and *Sniper Logic*.

Morgan McDermott

is a graduate of the University of Iowa and teaches creative writing at Adlai E. Stevenson High School. Recently, his short stories received awards from *The Nebraska Review, Dogwood*, the Ruth Hindman Foundation, *Mississippi Review, One Story, Short Story Journal*/Society for the Study of the Short Story, *River City*, the *Bellingham Review, New Millennium Writings, Bold Type, Phoebe*, and the Bridport Arts Centre in the U.K. He resides on the North Shore of Chicago with his wife, Wendy Parks.

Elizabeth Brinkley

received her MFA in Fiction from the University of Oregon. Her work has been published in the *Beloit Fiction Journal*, the *Seattle Weekly*, and other small publications. "Tinkerbell" is based on the first chapter of her novel-in-progress entitled, *Sweet Mary*. She has been awarded residencies at Hedgebrook, the Millay Colony for the Arts, and two scholarships to the Bread Loaf Writer's Conference. She currently serves as the fiction editor of *www.ChimeraReview.com*, an online literary journal. Elizabeth lives in Seattle, Washington, USA. She hopes her friend's Rottweiler, Tinkerbell, is alive and well and sunning himself by the pool in Palm Springs, California.

Freda Churches

lives in Denny, Stirlingshire. She has three grown up children, a degree in English from Stirling University, and a Masters in Creative Writing from Glasgow. Her work has been published in *Cencrastus*, *Chapman*, *Mslexia* and *Nerve Magazine*. She has received a bursary from The Scottish Arts Council and has had a story from her collection, *Lonely People*, read on BBC radio. Her novel, *The Caretaker's Daughter*, still needs a publisher to tend to it.

Teresa R Funke

is the author of *Remember Wake,* a novel based on a true story from WWII. She has worked as a researcher for PBS and several museums. She has published dozens of articles, short stories, and essays in numerous magazines and anthologies. Teresa is currently at work on the nonfiction book *We Can Do It: American Women's Stories from World War II* and a second novel. Born and raised in Boise, Idaho, she now lives with her husband and family in Colorado. Please visit her author website at *www.teresafunke.com*.

Virginia McRae

lives in a small town in the northeastern United States and earns her living as an independent editor of fiction and nonfiction for Manhattan publishing houses. She has twice won first prize in a lawyers' writing competition (once for a story on law and human rights in China) and has published poetry in literary journals. She has had a lifelong fascination with Chinese history and is completing a mystery novel set in ninth-century China.

Gina Ochsner

I live and work in Western Oregon. I try and write as much as the kids will allow and my husband can tolerate. This story is close to me because one night I dreamed I was on the ice with my dog, a big wolfy looking Siberian Huskie. We fell through a soft patch of ice and went crashing into the water. I squeezed my eyes closed and took a big gulp of water, hoping to hurry along the inevitable. That's when I noticed that the water wasn't cold. Still underwater, I opened my eyes and saw my dog swimming around in circles, having the time of his life.
This is the way stories come to me, through a series of happy accidents and bizarre overlaps, little collisions of life's charity.

Sean Lusk

Sean Lusk's short stories start in a dribble of time: a glass breaking into silence, a smile on a slapped face, the smell of whiskey on a baby's head. He searches for stories in African bars and Indian wells and English trains, but has lately discovered that stories, like the perfect morning, defy finding. Stories find us; they steal upon us when we're not looking, so that they are as invisible to us as we are to them. But by squeezing his eyes shut and listening very carefully with his left ear, Sean has recently heard the murmur of one or two.
Sean lives near Brighton, England and travels as much as possible.

Linda E Clopton

As a child, she played word games with her grandfather on his front porch in Alabama, where she learned that words are both precise and chameleon-like. Her work has appeared in literary journals and an anthology by Crossing Press. She received a PEN Syndicated Fiction award for a story subsequently published in the *San Francisco Chronicle* and *The Kansas City Star*. She has been a finalist for the Katherine Anne Porter prize and the River Oak/Hemingway award and received a residency fellowship to Hedgebrook Farm, where her story "Mazes" first began to take shape.

Sophie Spalding

lives on Dublin's northside with her husband and two young sons. She writes short stories and poetry and has published both in *The Electric Acorn*.

Editor's Choice
Janice Nabors Raiteri

Janice Nabors Raiteri's short stories have been published in *The Best of Carve, Potpourri,* and *The Algonquin Roundtable Review*. *Love Hater*, a screenplay she co-wrote with her husband, Charles, is set to shoot in Montreal this July. She lives in Oxford, Mississippi, and is about to complete the manuscript for her first novel.

Editor's Choice
Rosemary Jenkinson

was born in Belfast in 1967 and currently works in the Employment Agency. She studied Medieval Literature at Durham University and since then has had a variety of jobs including working as an astrologist for a magazine and teaching English in Greece, France, Poland and the Czech Republic.

Eoin O'Connor

was born 12 May 1970 in Nenagh, Co. Tipperary. Eoin has lived in
Galway and London and currently lives in Dublin where he works for
the Department of Agriculture. He is working on his first collection
of short stories.

Lara Fergus

was conceived on an ocean liner bound for Australia from London. She
grew up in the western suburbs of Sydney, and later dropped out of a
science degree to become a ballet dancer. She has been plagued by
such unreasonable ideas ever since. She spends most of her time in
transit.

Authors Who Reached the Final Shortlist

Ailbhe Slevin

Adrian Casey

Andrew Lloyd-Jones

Andrew Palmer

Ann Jolly

Aran Rafferty

Clare Birchall

Connie Chiu

Connla Stokes

Elizabeth Brinkley

Eoin O'Connor

Fiona Rintoul

Freda Churches

Gary Duggan

Geona Edwards

Gina Ochsner

Helena Close

Hester Casey

Hil Humby

Jacob Lee

Janice Nabors Raiteri

Jason Bellipanni

Jim Brannin

Jo Verity

Joan Halperin

Jocelyn Jane Cox

John Kachuba

Karen Meredith

Kate Rigby

Katy Darby

Kristi Gedeon

Lane Ashfeldt

Lara Fergus

Linda E Clopton

Mary Elizabeth Heard

Mia Gallagher

Morgan McDermott

Patrick Riordan

Paul Blaney

Ray Daly

Rosemary Jenkinson

Sarah Weir

Sean Lusk

Sean Mackel

Sophie Spalding

Teresa R Funke

V M Spreadborough

Virginia McRae

Details of the Annual Fish Short Story Prize

Judges for 2003/2004
To be appointed

Conditions:
Stories must not exceed 5,000 words. There is no minimum.
There are no restrictions on theme or style, we are looking for quality, unpublished work.
Name and address should not appear on the text, but on a separate sheet.
A fee of €15, (£11, US$15) for the first story is required, €10 (£8, US$10) per subsequent story. €10 per story for full-time students, pensioners and the unemployed. Cheques payable to Fish Publishing.
The judges' verdict is final. No correspondence will be entered into once work has been submitted.
If receipt of entry, notification of results, or any other information is needed, include a SAE or email address.
Stories will not be returned unless they are being critiqued.
Closing date 30th November, every year.
Results announced 17th March on our website.
Entry will be deemed as acceptance of these conditions.
No entry form is needed.

Send stories to:

Fish Short Story Prize,
Durrus, Bantry,
Co. Cork,
Ireland.

Honorary Patrons: *Roddy Doyle, Dermot Healy, Frank McCourt*

Prizes

First Prize:
€1,500

Second Prize:
One week at Anam Cara Writers' and Artists' Retreat.
Contact: Sue Booth-Forbes.
Address: Eyeries, The Beara Peninsula, Co. Cork, Ireland.
Tel: 00 353 (0)27 74441
E-Mail: anamcararetreat@eircom.net
Website: www.ugr.com/anamcararetreat/
Situated in one of the most rugged and beautiful parts of
Ireland overlooking Kenmare Bay, this is an ideal place to
write. Also to walk, swim, fish, read, or take a drink in the pubs
of the idyllic town of Eyeries. It is run by Sue Booth-Forbes,
who lends a personal touch to this unique set-up.

**The top 15 stories will be published in Fish's next
anthology,** and will be read by literary agents, including
Shirley Stewart, Geraldine Cooke and Merric Davidson.

.

Critique:
We offer a critique service for short stories. The critique will be
constructive, aimed at helping to improve both the story and the
writing in general. To avail of this service, send €45 (£35, $45) with
your story, and a SAE. If you are entering the story in the
competition include entry fee as well.